MIGHT AS WELL BE DEAD

Mark Goldblatt

PHOENIX PRESS LTD

Might as Well be Dead

Published 2023
First Edition
PHOENIX PRESS LTD
New Haven Publishing Children's Books Imprint
www.newhavenpublishingltd.com
newhavenpublishing@gmail.com

All Rights Reserved
The rights of Mark Goldblatt, as the author of this work, have been asserted in accordance with the Copyrights, Designs and Patents Act 1988.
No part of this book may be re-printed or reproduced or utilized in any form or by any electronic, mechanical or other means, now unknown or hereafter invented, including photocopying, and recording, or in any information storage or retrieval system, without the written permission of the
Authors and Publisher.

Cover Design illustration © Margot Holtman and Melissa Smock.

Copyright © 2023 Mark Goldblatt
All rights reserved
ISBN: 978-1-949515-51-0

Acknowledgments

Among those who contributed in subtle and conspicuous ways to this book are my publisher, Teddie Dahlin, my copy editor, Adrienne Kisner, my literary agent, Andy Ross, and my beloved safe harbor, Linda Helble and Barak. Lastly, of course, nothing contained in these pages would or could exist without John, Paul, George, and Ringo

Might as Well be Dead

"Limitless undying love which shines around me like
a million suns
It calls me on and on across the universe."
–the Beatles, "Across the Universe"

Might as Well be Dead

The first time I ever laid eyes on him, I was ninety-nine percent sure he wasn't real. It was three-thirty in the afternoon on a Wednesday. I was walking home after my last class at Talbot, and I noticed him across the street, walking in the opposite direction. He was hard to miss because he had hair down to his shoulders and wore a white sport jacket and white pants. That's not the sort of outfit guys wear in my neighborhood, not unless they're selling ice cream, and it was October, and too cold for ice cream, and there wasn't an ice cream truck in sight. But what made me sure, or almost sure, he wasn't real was that he had on a pair of wire-rimmed wizard glasses—which you definitely wouldn't wear, even if you *were* selling ice cream, unless you were selling it out of a cauldron. We locked eyes, and he stared me down; then he cracked up and gave me a comical wink. It was the kind of wink where you nod your head and wink at the same time, so there's no way to miss it.

That cracked *me* up, but it also made me feel weird, and I turned my head. Then, when I glanced back across the street, he was gone.

The next time I saw him was a couple of days later, on Friday morning. This time I was on my way to Talbot. He was standing on the corner of the next block, too far off for me to read the expression on his face, but he had on the same white suit and wizard glasses. When he saw me look up, he did a quick dance, shuffling his feet back and forth and rocking his arms side to side. After that, for no reason, he took off running. I started to run after him. I ran about ten steps, but then I stopped. I rested my hands on my knees and took long, deep breaths. What was I doing? Why was I chasing after a guy who I was ninety-nine percent sure was a hallucination?

I mulled that over for like a half minute until I came up with an answer: because that meant there was still a one percent chance that he *wasn't* a hallucination, that he was a real guy in a white suit and wizard glasses, hanging around my neighborhood. Unreal or real. I needed to know, either way, in order to figure out if I was going crazy…which there was a ninety-nine percent chance I was. So it made sense to chase him down and find out what was going on.

By the time I decided to keep running, he was long gone.

The third time I saw him was that Sunday. Except I heard him before I saw him. I was standing at the end of my block, waiting for the sun to go down, and he came up behind me and said, "So you're a Jewish?"

I spun around and jumped backward. Ninety-nine percent isn't a hundred percent, so you don't want to let down your guard. Whether he was unreal or real though, he seemed pretty harmless. He was closer to me than he'd ever gotten, true, but he wasn't breathing down my neck. He was keeping his distance. Unless of course he *wasn't* keeping his distance because he only existed inside my head.

Plus, not to get dramatic, the street was deserted. It wasn't quite night, even though not much was left of the afternoon. He must have realized, in any case, that he'd scared the daylights out of me because once I jumped backward, he backed off even more. He held up his hands with his palms forward. He was smiling at me, and he slid his glasses down his nose so that I could look him in the eye.

"That's a weird way to say it," I said.

"Say what?"

"You said 'a Jewish.' I'm not a Jewish."

"You're not?"

"I'm a Jew. I'm Jewish. I'm not *a* Jewish."

"Point taken. Does it bother you, son?"

"No," I said. "Why would it bother me?"

"I've got nothing against it. I'm just noticing it as a matter of fact."

"How did you know that I was Jewish?"

"I'm up on the scuttlebutt," he said. "Got to keep on top of things."

"You've got a funny accent."

"Do I? I was thinking the same of you."

"Where did you come from?" I asked.

"How old are you?" he shot back.
"Why does that matter?"
"Eye for an eye, as your people say."
"That's not what that means," I said.
"Nevertheless…"
"Fine. I'm thirteen. Where did you come from?"
"Here, there, and wherever you like," he said.
"Where's that?"
"Nowhere in particular."
"You're not going to tell me?"
"Tell you what?"
"Where you were born," I said.
"The land of kingly queens, union jacks, and other assorted playing cards."

He brought his right hand to his forehead, then snapped it back to his side.

"You're from Queens?"

He shook his head. "Jesters all the way down, son. Jesters all the way down."

"C'mon, I told you I was thirteen. What happened to an eye for an eye?"

"That's not what that means," he said, "or so they want you to believe."

Neither of us spoke for a few seconds.

It felt awkward, standing there, on the deserted street, with neither of us talking. "I've got to get home."

"Do you now?"

"No, I mean, I *really* do. My dad is—"

"Well, what's stopping you then?"

I glanced over my shoulder at my house. "I live right over there, the second house."

That made him laugh. "Yes, well maybe in the next life you'll make the first house."

I had to step over cardboard boxes of my mom's stuff when I got home. It had been a month and a half since she'd left, and she called me a couple of times a week, asking when my dad was going to pack up the rest of her stuff, the books and records and papers, and the clothes she hadn't worn in like forever yet still wanted. But I knew the real reason she kept calling was to check in on us. She never wanted to talk to my dad, naturally. I kept my voice down when she called because I knew that if he knew she was on the phone, it would have wrecked him. Or wrecked him more. He was sitting in his bathrobe at that moment, in a rocking chair, right in the middle of the mess, rocking back and forth. He had that look on his face he gets when he's *done*, even if he's not finished. Like, he's done as much as he's going to do, even if there's still more to go. His cheeks were puffed with air, and he was whistling the air out of his mouth, like a tea kettle that's come to a boil, except softer. He needed a shave. He didn't shave as often as he did before my mom left.

Pretty much whenever she called, she reminded me that I had to look after my dad, that he needed me, and that she needed me to look after him. She was right, too. You just had to see him sitting in that rocking chair, with his bathrobe open to the waist, with boxes of her stuff at his feet, to know she was right. He was sitting there, breathing out like a tea kettle, like it was a coin flip whether he was *ever* getting out of that chair.

You know what? If not for me, maybe he *wasn't* ever getting out of that chair.

"Hey, David," my dad said, as I hung up my jacket.

"Yeah?"

"I guess we should probably order dinner."

"Chinese?"

"If that's what you're tasting," he said.

He slid his phone out of the pocket of his robe and called for food.

Sunday night was dull...unless you counted the conversation with the hallucination as a night thing instead of a late afternoon thing. Or a sundown thing, which was how I counted it. Sundown felt like a more logical time for it to happen. You're hungry and tired and kind of used up, so that's when you get caught between what's real and what's not real. After dinner, though, I was fine. But Sunday night was flat-out dull. Nothing was on TV, or nothing I wanted to watch. (It had been over a month since I quit TikTok, Instagram, and Snapchat because they're time sucks, and because people want to know your business.) I got into bed at nine-thirty and stared at the ceiling. There's a streetlamp about a hundred feet from my house, and the light from it comes through the slats of the blinds on my window; it makes a light ladder on the opposite wall, so my bedroom never gets too dark. It's the kind of room where you can work up a good ceiling-stare if you're in the mood, and that night I was in the mood. My dad was crashing on the couch, which he did more and more. Sometimes he'd wake up in the middle of the night, trudge upstairs, and spend the rest of the night in his bed. But other times, he stayed downstairs. It killed his back when he spent the entire night on the couch, which made him late for work. He owned a dry cleaners on Francis Lewis Boulevard. He had a guy who opened for him, so it wasn't the end of the world if he rolled in an hour late. But it still didn't look good. What could you do though?

He was my dad. He was going through stuff.

That was what I was thinking, staring at the ceiling, when a gust of wind thumped against the window. I glanced over at it…and the guy from the street was standing there. Next to the window.

Inside my room.

I gasped at the sight of him and pulled the blanket over my head, which was like the dumbest thing you could do, if you think about it. It's the kind of thing a three-year-old kid would do.

I lay there with my head under the blanket for half a minute, reminding myself that he wasn't real. Ninety-nine percent. Meanwhile, nothing happened. It took half a minute, in other words, to go from feeling scared to feeling dumb.

Then I poked my head out from under the blanket.

He was sitting, cross-legged, on the floor.

"Shhh," he said, smiling.

"You're not real, are you?"

"You're a cheeky one!"

"But you're not," I said. "No offense."
"What's real nowadays?"
"I'm real."
"Then you've got nothing to worry about."
"How did you get in my room?" I asked.
"Came in through the window, I guess."
"Why?"
"I was hovering outside, and I noticed that the window was open."
"What do you mean, you were hovering?"
"You know. *Hovering*." He shrugged.
"You mean like floating in the air?"
"That's the only place you can get a hover going nowadays."
"You were floating in the air—"
"Hovering!"
"You were hovering in the air, and you came through the window?"
"That's my story," he said, "and I'm sticking to it."
"But the window is shut."
"Well, that changes things!"
"So you couldn't have hovered through the window," I said.
"The entire story sounds bloody unlikely, come to mention it."
"It doesn't sound *unlikely*," I said. "It sounds totally *impossible*."
"Well, then, maybe I'm *not* real. Maybe you're dreaming."
"But I'm not dreaming!"

"Ah, but what if you're dreaming you're not dreaming?"

"How could that be?"

"Happens all the time. Half of life is dreaming you're not dreaming."

"What's the other half?"

"Waking up," he said, "and we all know what a drag that is."

He began to laugh, and I laughed too.

"Then you admit I'm right. You admit you're not real."

"I'm not saying you're right, and I'm not saying you're wrong. I'm saying whichever it is, I'm not the boogie man. I applied for the job, you know, but I couldn't boogie."

"Why not?"

"Had on my blues shoes," he said. "Can't boogie with your blues shoes."

"I don't know what that means."

"It means you've got to have the right tools for the job, son. The right tools. There's the key…."

The next thing I remember was opening my eyes. It was Monday morning. The first thing I did was glance around the room, looking for the guy. Then I got out of bed, walked over to the window, and pulled up the blinds. The window was shut tight. The guy *couldn't* have gotten in through the window. He *couldn't* have been real. Whether or not I'd dreamed the conversation the night before, the guy I was seeing wasn't real. There was no other explanation. It wasn't ninety-nine percent. It was a hundred percent. He wasn't real. I knew it for sure now. I'd know it the next time I saw him.

It was a relief.

I decided not to think about him, which was hard to do at first, but I texted my friend Hector Caban, and we started going back and forth about the Mets and Jets, and before long, the unreal guy was the last thing on my mind. I was still texting in the kitchen ten minutes later, finishing off a couple of unfrosted strawberry Pop Tarts and guzzling a glass of skim milk. I felt bad afterward; they were the last two Pop Tarts in the pantry, which meant my dad would have to scrounge for breakfast when he woke up. But I was *starved*. Still, if I'd thought about my dad, I would've left him one.

I started a new grocery list on the notepad stuck to the refrigerator and put Pop Tarts and milk at the top.

Before I left, I headed back upstairs and pushed open the door to my dad's room. He was still in bed, asleep on top of the covers. The overhead light was on, which meant he'd slept with it on. I leaned into the room, trying to decide if I should wake him up. He had his left arm bent across his face. The stubble on his chin was dark and thick. I decided to let him sleep, but as I turned to walk out, the floor creaked. That woke him up. His arm came off his face, and he looked at me in a weird way through the slits of his eyes, like he was figuring out who I was. Then, a second later, he let out a yawn.

"Morning already?"

I nodded. "I'm about to leave."

"You washed yourself good?"

"Yeah."

"Then off you go," he said.

The unreal guy was leaning on a parked car in front of my house. He smiled at me as soon as I stepped out the front door.

I smiled back at him. "You're not a dream, but you're not real."

"Says who?"

"I'm looking at the thing logically," I said. "You *can't* be real."

"We're doing logic, eh? So if I'm not real, that must mean..."

"You're a hallucination."

"And...?"

"I'm going crazy," I said.

Saying it out loud felt weird. But you know what? Right after I said it, I thought: *Whatever*. Might as well roll with it.

"What's your name?" I asked.

He had to think for a second. "Winston."

"Did you just make that up?"

"If I made up a name, I'd come up with something better than Winston."

"Winston is a good name," I said. "It's random, but it's not *too* random."

"You're a gentleman to say so."

"What's your last name?"

He thought again, then said, "Ono."

"Oh no?"

"What's the skin off your nose?"

"C'mon!"

"It's nothing to get hung up about."

"You're not going to tell me?" I asked.

He shrugged at me, so I shrugged back at him. He leaned back against the parked car. I figured that was the end of the conversation. I put in my ear buds and started to walk to school. It was a half mile walk straight along Jewel Avenue to Talbot Middle School. Most of the time, I could do it in three or four songs.

After a couple of blocks, though, I got the sense that I wasn't alone. I glanced over my right shoulder, and Winston was behind me. He was maybe thirty feet back.

I stopped, and he stopped.

I took out my ear buds and walked back to him. "Are you following me?"

"Yes," he said.

"Why?"

"I thought you might lead me to a place of interest."

"I'm just going to school."

"Jewish school?"

"You mean Hebrew school?"

"Where you learn the secret handshakes," he said.

"I don't know any secret handshakes."

"What about secret milkshakes? I could go for one."

"I don't know any of those either," I said.

"Aye, son, they've trained you well."

"I don't go to Hebrew School. I'm just going to regular school."

Might as Well be Dead

"You don't want me to come, then?"

"*No*, I don't want you to come! Why would I want you to come?"

He put his hands over his heart. "You wound me to the quick!"

"That's not what I mean. I just think it would be pretty weird."

"Ah."

"Don't you?"

"I see your point...what's your name again?"

"My name is David," I said. "David Salmon."

"Salmon, did you say? Sounds fishy to me."

"Yeah, that's maybe the millionth time I've heard that joke."

"It's a cross to bear," he said. "Or don't they teach you that in Jewish School?"

"*Hebrew* School! And what did I just tell you?"

He shrugged, then pivoted on his heels and strode off in the other direction.

Hector was waiting at the fire hydrant. It was *our* hydrant. It got to be ours because it was where we'd first met. That was the first day of sixth grade, so I'd known him for over a year. The first time I laid eyes on him, he was hurdling the hydrant. He did it over and over; he was in his own world. I stopped and watched. He was grabbing the round gray cap of the hydrant with his palms and vaulting to the other side. It wasn't hard to do. But his shoulders were shaking. It took me a couple of seconds to realize he was nervous. He was so nervous that he didn't even notice I was standing there, watching him.

Then, at once, he saw me and took a step backward. He stumbled off the curb and fell onto his backside in the street. His glasses went flying off his face. I rushed forward and helped him up. Then, as he dusted himself off, I got his glasses. As he slid them back onto his nose, I said, "Smooth move, Ex-Lax."

That cracked him up, and afterwards we became friends.

It was hard to believe the guy waiting for me at the hydrant was the same guy I'd met that day. He was a half foot taller, and he had contact lenses instead of glasses. The girls in our homeroom were crazy for him. They sometimes rushed up behind us in the hallway and started conversations. But he never said more than a few sentences back; I figured he was too nervous. I didn't talk to them either, since it was obvious who they were interested in.

"You sure took your sweet time," he called to me.

I shrugged. "I didn't realize you were in a hurry."

"You know we've got a history quiz second period, right?"

"I know."

"Do you know who Thomas Paine was?" Hector asked.

"I know he was friends with Thomas Jefferson."

"What did he write?"

"The Declaration of Independence."

"Not Jefferson! Paine! What did Thomas Paine write?"

Might as Well be Dead

"I don't know," I said.

"He wrote *Common Sense*, and you're doomed."

"How do you know that'll even be on the quiz?"

"I *don't* know," Hector said. "But it's in the book."

I shrugged again. "Well, now I know Thomas Paine wrote *Common Sense*. You can stop worrying. If that question comes up, I'm prepared."

"What about the rest of it?"

"You just told me I'm doomed." I smiled at him. "So let's see what happens."

"Who wrote the pamphlet *Common Sense*?" turned out to be the second question on the history quiz. I got it right. I got the other nine questions wrong, and Mrs. Clark wrote the number "10" at the top of my answer sheet. She could have written "F," but that would have been more respectable, so she wrote "10"—just to make it sting. It's hard to get a ten out of a hundred on a quiz; it has to be a certain kind of quiz. If it's multiple choice, you're going to get higher than a ten just by guessing, and if it's an essay test, you're going to get higher than a ten just by writing *something*, even if it makes no sense, because the teacher will feel bad for you. You can only get a ten if it's a short answer quiz, and there's no wiggle room, which was what our history quiz was.

Actually, I knew a couple of answers, but I left them blank. The ninth question was: "Who was George Washington's vice president?" I knew the right answer was John Adams, but I said Thomas Jefferson because by then I realized I was going to fail, and I thought: *Screw it, I might as well go down in flames.* Plus, I knew that Aaron Burr shot Alexander Hamilton, which was question six. But what difference did it make if I knew the names of famous dead guys: Paine, Jefferson, Adams, Burr, Hamilton, or even George Washington? It was no skin off my nose. You should've seen the look Mrs. Clark shot me as she handed back the graded answer sheet. She rolled her eyes, and I smiled at her. When she saw I was smiling, she shook her head. That was the end of it.

Like I said, no skin off my nose.

Hector stared at my answer sheet after class. "What did I tell you?"

"You told me I was doomed."

"You got a ten. I mean, a ten. Who gets a ten? That's impossible."

"*Almost* impossible," I said.

"You're right. It's *almost* impossible."

"That's my point."

"Yes, *almost* impossible and impossible are different. Satisfied?"

"Plus, here I am, talking to you, so it turns out I wasn't doomed."

"Fine, Mr. Literal. But isn't your dad going to be pissed?"

"I don't think he's too worried about my history grade," I said.

"You know," Hector said, "that's not very nice."

I laughed. "Yeah, but who told you I was nice?"

Might as Well be Dead

Winston caught up with me during my walk home after school. I slowed down as he hustled up the block and waited while he caught his breath. It took a while. He was wheezing pretty hard. I kind of figured he'd turn up; I'd noticed him during lunch period when I glanced out the cafeteria window, so I knew he was lurking around.

"I saw you during lunch period."

"Did you?"

"Yes," I said.

"Maybe you were hallucinating."

"You were standing across the street from the school yard, pacing back and forth."

"That *does* sound like me," he said. "Been a pacer my whole life. Nothing to be done about it, I'm afraid."

"You were in front of the bodega."

"What was I doing?"

"Nothing much," I said. "You took out a pack of cigarettes from your jacket pocket, took a cigarette out of the pack, and stared at it. You didn't smoke it. You only stared at it. Then, for no reason, you flicked it into the gutter. Then you tossed the rest of the pack into a garbage can."

"Those things will kill you."

"My mom used to smoke. But she quit."

"Good for her!"

"Why are you following me?" I asked.

"*There's* a straightforward question!"

"What's the answer?"

"It's a mystery wrapped in an enigma."

"Meaning?"

"Meaning I don't quite know," he said.

"How could you not know something like that?"

"Strange thing. It's right on the tip of my tongue."

"So?"

He squeezed his eyes closed, then opened them. "No, sorry. It's gone."

"That's it?"

"I think maybe there's something I'm supposed to set right," he said.

"What kind of thing?"

"Complete blank on that."

"Great."

"But I'm pretty sure I need your help."

That perked up my interest. "*My* help?"

"Yeah."

"You know you only exist in my head, right?"

"Well, that's news to me," he said. "It's pretty roomy though."

"Is that supposed to be a joke?"

"I never joke with the landlord." He looked at me expectantly.

"All right, let's drop it," I said.

"Done!"

"Now back to this thing you need to set right…."

"Right!"

"What else do you know about it?"

"Just that you're supposed to help me," he said.

"Hmm. That's not a lot to go on."

"That's what makes it a mystery."

"Yeah, but—"

"What say we pool our resources?" he said.

"Fine by me."

Might as Well be Dead

He clenched his fist in the air. "There's the stuff!"

After that, there was a long pause.

Then, at once, he gave me a sneaky look. "Anyway, I figure you can use a distraction. Am I right, or am I right?"

"What's that supposed to mean?"

"No offense! No offense! Water under the bridge, *et cetera*. What did you learn in school today?"

"I learned that Thomas Paine wrote *Common Sense*."

"Pain in the arse, if you ask me."

"'Arse' means 'ass' where you come from?"

"You bet your ass it does. But does a fish have an arse? *That's* the catch of the day!"

"You mean like a *salmon*, right?" I said.

"Watch out, son. They'll hate you if you're clever."

"So…"

"What's on your mind?"

"Just one more thing, and you can't get offended."

"Oh, I don't like the sound of that," he said.

"Since you're not real…"

"Here we go again!"

"I was wondering what would happen if I tried to touch you."

"I'd be on the phone to my lawyer in a minute," he said. "He's one of your tribe too if I'm not mistaken. You may even know the git. Cases full of law books. Diplomas on the wall. Cease and desist! Cease and desist! I'm telling you, he's a shark."

I gave him a serious look, which quieted him down.

"What I mean is," I said, "if I tried to touch your hand, it wouldn't be there, would it?"

"You want to touch my hand?"

"You're saying I *could* touch your hand?"

"Have at it, my boy!"

He put out his hand, and I walked forward. I hesitated for a second, but then reached out. I took hold of his hand, and he closed his fingers around mine. His hand felt cold and clammy, like a dead guy's hand; it made my hand feel cold and clammy. But it felt real. It felt as real as mine did. So maybe he *was* there. Except not there. Like a ghost, I guess, but also like a zombie. Except not the flesh-chewing kind. Just the weird kind.

"Convinced?" he said.

"Yeah, I guess."

"We can stop the touchy-feely then?"

I let go of his hand and took a step back. "Sorry, I just—"

"No attachments! It'll wreck your peace of mind!"

My phone started to vibrate as soon as I walked through the front door of my house. My mom's photo came up underneath her cell number.

"What is it?" I asked.

"That's a fine hello!"

"Hello, mom."

"You sound mad."

"I'm not mad," I said. "I'm just curious why you're calling in the middle of the day."

"I just wanted to hear your voice, David. I miss you. Is that so hard to understand?"

"I miss you too. But you're the one who—"
"You *are* mad."
"I'm not mad, mom. Really and truly, I'm not."
"Because I would have stayed if I could've—"
"You don't have to explain it again," I said.
"It's just so good to hear your voice."
She started to sob after she said that.
"Dad misses you too, you know. He's a mess. You should see how he—"
"Yes, I know that, David. But he's a good man. He'll pull through for you."
"Your stuff is all over the place. It's like mostly boxed, but it's scattered."
"Oh, my! That's not healthy."
"I know," I said.
"It's not as if I need any of it right now. But he should get it out of the house."
"I'll work on him."
"He's a good man," she said.
"You already said that."
"It bears repeating. He just needs looking after."
We talked about stuff for a few more minutes, nothing that mattered, just stuff. After we hung up, I slid off my shoes and took deep breaths. I headed upstairs to my bedroom. About a minute later, Hector texted, and we started going back and forth about the history quiz. The guy wouldn't let it drop! I kept telling him to think about the big picture, about how failing one history quiz in seventh grade wasn't going to make the slightest difference in the big picture. But he came back at me. He said that if you followed that logic, what's the point of

studying at all? Why not blow off seventh grade? And eighth? And ninth? Sooner or later, the small picture *becomes* the big picture!

I had to admit it; he had a point.

"I promise," I said. "I'll pass the next quiz."

My dad called around six-thirty to say he was working late, so I ordered a pizza and ate two slices. I wrapped the rest in foil so it would be waiting for him when he came home. (If I hadn't just told my mom I was going to look after him, I probably would have left the last four slices in the delivery box.) He still wasn't home at ten o'clock though, so I washed up, brushed my teeth, and climbed into bed. I half-expected Winston to turn up in my room—which made no sense, because if I could feel him, how could he get into my room? Except, of course, he'd already done it once. I figured the only way he was going to turn up was if I fell asleep and dreamed about him, which, come to think of it, *had* to be what had happened the night before.

I closed my eyes and pulled up the blankets to my neck.

Half an hour later, I heard a set of keys jangling outside. Then I heard the front door creak open, and my dad's footsteps downstairs. He called my name, but I didn't answer him. He came upstairs and slid open the door of my room, but I lay still with my eyes shut. I wasn't mad. I just didn't want to get out of bed and keep him company as he ate the rest of the pizza. It was too depressing.

He headed back downstairs, and I opened my eyes.

I glanced over at the window. No sign of Winston. Then I thought about the fact that I was lying in bed, looking for him, and I laughed at myself. I rolled over on my side, faced the wall, and thought: *Even if I'm not crazy, I'm nuts.*

My dad was sitting at the table, already dressed for work, when I came downstairs on Tuesday morning. There were slices of toast stacked on a small plate in the middle of the table, next to a stick of butter, and jars of grape jelly and orange marmalade. He was smiling at me in a weird way, kind of proud but kind of guilty.

"Good morning," he said.

"You made breakfast?"

"You think it got here on its own?"

"What happened to Pop Tarts?"

"I was thinking maybe we should take a break," he said. "I got turkey-sausage links in the freezer. You want me to heat them in the microwave?"

"Really?"

"Yeah."

"Okay then," I said.

He jumped up from his chair and headed for the refrigerator. As he brushed past me, I got a whiff of liquor from his sports jacket. He hardly ever drank, so I was thinking maybe I was wrong, but a few minutes later, when he came back to the table with sausages steaming on a plate, I could smell the meat and the liquor. The combination of the two smelled like the inside of a headache.

He pushed two of the sausage links onto my plate and the other two onto his, then sat back down.

"Dig in," he said.

"Why are you doing this?"

"Doing what?"

"Fixing breakfast," I said.

"Because life goes on."

"Well, yeah—"

"Look, David, we took a shot. We took a real hard shot to the jaw, both of us. We got knocked down. Now we got to get back up. We got to get off our butt and get back in the fight."

"Why don't you just say arse"?

"What?"

"Instead of butt, why don't you say *arse*?"

He gave me a look.

"My point being," he said, "it's enough already! You understand what I'm getting at? Life goes on. It just does."

"So you're going to finish packing up mom's stuff?"

"That's not the point," he said. "That's, like, an outside thing."

"But it's inside. We've been climbing over those boxes since—"

"We got to get our *minds* right, David. That's the main thing."

Before I left for school, I peeked through the living room curtains a few times, looking for Winston. My dad was getting ready to leave too, and we kept crisscrossing, and after my third peek through the curtains, he began to laugh. "You expecting the Spanish Inquisition?"

"Who's that?"

"What are you doing, David?"

"Just checking the weather."

"It's the same as it was two minutes ago."

"Do you think it'll rain?" I asked.

"Never know."

"I mean, it's pretty sunny right now. I don't think it's going to rain."

"Never know."

He was still smiling at me as I headed out the door.

I looked up and down the block for Winston, but he wasn't there. Out of the corner of my eye, I caught sight of my dad peeking through the curtains at me, so I started walking to school. Every block or so, I glanced over my shoulder to see if Winston was following me. But he wasn't. I put in my ear buds and put him out of my mind.

I got to the fire hydrant before Hector and waited five minutes for him. Then, at last, he showed up. He was with a girl. She had big blue eyes, but they were maybe a quarter of an inch too far apart; the extra space gave her a delicate look, like a bird. Her hair was long and Goth-white and as straight and stringy as spaghetti, with a streak on one side dyed the same shade of blue as her eyes. It was like she wanted them to match.

Hector shot me a glance before he said a word, like, *Hey, don't blame me....*

Then he said, "This is my friend David. Okay? David, this is Minnie."

I half-waved at her. "Hi, Minnie."

She waved back but didn't speak.

"Minnie moved onto my block, and her mom and my mom are friends."

"Do you like pralines?" Minnie said.

"What are pralines?"

"*What are pralines*!" She shuddered. "Just the most delicious things ever!"

"All right, but what are they?"

"They're like a combination of a cookie and a candy, except much better."

"What are they made out of?" I asked, not because I was interested but because she seemed to want to tell me.

"The main ingredients are nuts and sugar. But people do different things with them. Like Belgian pralines are dipped in chocolate and have a cream filling, but French pralines are harder since they use almonds, and American pralines are as soft as Belgians but not dipped in chocolate. Americans are the best, and I'm not saying that because I'm prejudiced. They use hazelnuts. I *love* hazelnuts in pralines. Hazelnut pralines are the best things in the solar system. I can't say if they're the best things in the universe since you never know what's out there. You know, there's billions and billions of other galaxies. But definitely, in our solar system, you got to go with hazelnut pralines."

"They sound pretty good," I said.

"I could make you some!"

"C'mon," Hector broke in, "he's not interested in pralines."

"I don't know. Maybe I am."

Minnie smiled at me. "So, your last name is Salmon, right?"

"Yeah."

"You must get a lot of fish jokes."

"Only billions and billions of them," I said.

"Then I'll have to come up with a good one, a real doozy."

"Is Minnie your real name?"

"Nope. My real name is Minerva. Minerva S. Drugas."

"You're putting me on," I said.

"Nope. Minerva S. Drugas."

"What does the S stand for?"

"I'll never tell," she said. "Ask me about my hair though."

"What about your hair?"

"What do you notice about it? The most unusual thing?"

"You mean the blue streak?"

"It's called a *highlight*, for your information," she said.

"Isn't a streak the same thing as a highlight?"

"If you don't know what you're taking about, maybe."

"All right, it's a highlight."

"Aren't you even curious why I got a *blue* highlight?"

"I'm sure you had a reason," I said.

"Yes, I did, and that reason was because my parents got a divorce, and my mom and I had to move, and I got sad about it, and I felt blue, like I needed a change, so I got a blue highlight, and after that I felt okay again. You'd be surprised what a blue highlight can do for you."

"And you're telling me this because…?"

"Because Hector told me about your mom," she said, "and I know it's not *exactly* the same thing, but I thought maybe you'd want a highlight. It doesn't have to be blue; it can be whatever color you want. I can do it for you. I know how. You name the color, and I can do a highlight."

As she was talking, I caught sight of Hector, off to the side, waving his arms. He looked like an umpire making a safe sign, telling her not to go there. But I didn't mind. I kind of liked how she came straight at me, not walking on eggshells.

"Let me think about it," I said.

"Or maybe you could do aroma therapy. I tried it a couple of times. I don't know how much I believe in it, but I like the smells."

"How is smelling smells therapy?"

She looked me up and down, then said, "Stephanie."

"What?"

"My middle name is Stephanie."

"I thought you said you'd never tell," I said.

"I trust you. Besides, Hector already knows."

I turned to Hector, and he was cracking up.

Then the three of us walked the rest of the way to Talbot.

As soon as we passed through the double doors, Minnie spun toward me and put out her right hand. We shook hands; she had a firm grip, like she meant it, and one of her nails dug slightly into my palm. Afterward, she turned and headed off to her homeroom on the far end of the third floor.

Hector waited until she was out of earshot to apologize…for the first time. About six apologies later, I cut him off.

"It's not a big deal," I said.

"The thing is, my mom and her mom are friends, so I *have* to be nice to her."

"Why didn't you mention her before?"

"Because I figured it was just a neighborhood thing," he said. "Like I had to be nice to her around the block. But then my mom said she wasn't making friends at school, so maybe I could introduce her to mine. I didn't think she'd be like *that* though. I mean, she doesn't even know you—"

"She's all right."

"She must have been saving up that stuff about pralines."

"Who knows? Maybe they're exceptional."

"Plus, the other thing, about your mom—"

"Let it go, Hector," I said. "It's fine. I'm fine."

We headed to homeroom on the second floor, but our teacher, Mrs. Pang, caught me by the arm before I could get to my desk. She held onto me and whispered in my ear, "Mr. Ivan wants to talk to you."

Mr. Ivan…the guidance counselor.

I let out a deep breath and headed back out into the hall.

Mr. Ivan's office was next to the principal's, near the main entrance on the first floor. That meant I had to retrace my steps, and when I got there, the office was locked. I stood in front of the door for several seconds, staring at the doorknob, as if staring at it would make it less locked, and then a deep voice called to me.

"Mr. Salmon!"

Mr. Ivan, a tall black guy in a sports jacket and red sneakers, was jogging toward me.

"Mrs. Pang told me to come to your—"

"I know," he said. "I'm running late."

"Should I go back to my homeroom?"

He leaned past me and unlocked the door. "No, just wait inside. I'll be back in a few minutes."

Then he jogged back in the direction he'd come from, and I slid open the door to his office.

Winston was sitting cross-legged on a couch inside.

"Oh, come on!" I said, as much to myself as to him. "What are you doing here?"

He jumped up and thrust out both of his arms, as if they were handcuffed together. "Life without parole. My future's all behind me. But there's still hope for you, young trout! With the right kind of schooling, the tide's the limit!"

"It's not funny," I said. "You're going to get me in trouble."

He ushered me over to the couch and sat me down. "You're in the counselor's office. How much more trouble—"

"I could wind up in the principal's office."

"It's just one door down. He's got a much nicer couch."

"How do you know?"

"My spies are everywhere," he said.

"What are you going to do when Mr. Ivan gets back?"

"Evaporate, most likely."

That took me by surprise. "Then you're *not* real?"

"Says you! Real people evaporate all the time."

"Name one," I said.

"That invisible bloke."

"Who?"

"The invisible bloke."

"You mean *The Invisible Man*? Like in the movie?"

"You see my point...."

The office door swung open, and Mr. Ivan came in. I jumped up from the couch as he shut the door, and when I when I sat back down, Winston was gone. I was sitting alone on the couch.

Completely crazy, I said to myself.

"So," Mr. Ivan said, as he sat behind his desk, "I gather history isn't your strongest subject nowadays."

"Oh, you mean the quiz?"

"It's not like you to neglect your schoolwork, David."

It *wasn't* like me to neglect my schoolwork, but how would he know? He had never spoken to me before. I sized him up. The top button of his shirt was undone, and he had a thin gold chain around his neck. His hair was cut into a thick, high fade, which made him look even taller than he was, which was pretty tall.

"I didn't neglect it," I said. "I just couldn't remember the answers."

"Were you distracted? Do you want to re-take the test?"

"No, it's nothing like that. I just had an off day. That's it."

"Are you sure?"

"Yeah, I'm sure."

"All right, then."

He stood up.

"That's all?"

"I wanted you to know that you've got a support system," he said.

"Does that mean I can go back to my homeroom?"

"Unless you want to talk for a bit, in which case I'm here to listen."

"I'd rather go back to my homeroom."

"You can stop by anytime," he said.

Just like that, he walked me to the door and let me out.

Winston caught up with me again on the walk home after school. But not as near the school as last time; it wasn't until I was six blocks from my house that I heard his footsteps. We walked side by side for half a minute. Neither of us spoke, which felt unnatural. Then he started to whistle, which made it worse. When I couldn't take it anymore, I said, "Nothing bad happened."

"That's a relief!"

"Are you sure about that?"

"About what?" he asked.

"Are you sure you're not *trying* to get me in trouble?"

"Who? *Moi*?"

"Yes, you."

"Slanderous charge! You think *that's* why I'm here?"

"Except you're not here," I said.

He gestured toward the sidewalk. "Tell it to that shadow."

Sure enough, our two shadows were walking side by side.

"What does that prove?"

"It proves I'm blocking the sun. It's not going through me."

I thought about that for a few seconds. "Not necessarily."

"How do you reckon?"

"Maybe the shadow's not there either. Maybe you and your shadow are both in my head."

He narrowed his eyes at me. "Quite the deduction, Holmes."

"Think about it," I said. "You're a grown man, right? There's no possible way you could have walked into a middle school with nobody noticing. You'd have to get a pass at the security desk. But you didn't get a pass. You just turned up in Mr. Ivan's office. Oh, and then you disappeared without going out the door."

"I'm pretty stealthy," he said.

"Nobody is *that* stealthy."

"You're saying—what?"

"You're a hallucination," I said. "I just proved it. You're in my head. You're not real."

"Oh, yeah? Well, what about—"

"You're a hallucination I can see *and* feel. But you're still a hallucination. There's no other way to look at it."

"I beg to differ," he said.

"I'm listening…."

He scratched his chin as if he were thinking deep thoughts. "Well, I could be a spirit. Or else a demon. That's always possible. Or maybe I'm just a guy who's learned how to duck in and out from time to time."

"I don't believe in any of that."

"There are more things in heaven and earth than are dreamt of in your philosophy."

"What does that even mean?"

"Aha!"

"What?"

"If you don't know what it means, and I said it, how could I be your hallucination?"

He had a point.

"All right," I said, "let's suppose that you are a spirit."

"Whoa, whoa, whoa! Why are we ruling out demon?"

"You're *not* a demon."

"You're only saying that because I'm a charmer."

"Trust me, I'm not."

"What if I rip off my face and let out my tentacles?"

"Be my guest."

"Well, I could, you know. But I'm not in the mood."

That made me laugh. "What's this thing we're supposed to be doing together?"

"Come again?"

"This thing we're supposed to set right, what is it?"

"I'm still working on that."

Might as Well be Dead

Minnie texted me right before I got into bed. I didn't realize the text was from her at first; the number came up, and the entire message was: "Busy? M." I stared at it for like ten seconds before I figured out who "M" was.

"No," I texted back. "Just tired."
"Here's the thing. I like you."
"I like you too."
"I think you're cute."

I got a weird feeling in my gut. My fingers stiffened up.

Another text came through. "Don't you think I'm cute?"

"Yes," I wrote back.
"Are you only saying that because I made you say it?"
"No, I think it because it's true."
"Really?"
"Yes, really," I wrote.
"You don't think I'm a chatterbox?"
"You do talk a lot."

I waited for a reply; none came.

"But not too much," I wrote.
"You're sweet."
"Thanks."
"But I am a chatterbox. You should always be honest."
"I agree."
"I think what you need is a happily-ever-after."
"What's a happily-ever-after?"
"You know, at the end of a movie, how things work out, and the guy and the girl wind up together? That's a

happily-ever-after. It's the last thing you see before the screen goes dark, and you see the names of the director and actors."

"What about THE END?" I wrote.

"Not all movies end with THE END. Sometimes they just go dark without the words."

"Plus, the guy and the girl don't always wind up together."

"I didn't say every movie was a happily-ever-after, did I?"

"You kind of did."

"Well, that's not what I meant. But don't you WANT a happily-ever-after?"

"Not if I have to force it."

"Do you want to keep texting or stop now?" she wrote.

I thought it over. "Stop now."

"But it's all right if I text you again, right?"

"Yes."

"Are you going to put my name into your contacts?"

"Yes."

"Are you going to put it in as Minnie or Minerva?"

"Whichever you want."

"Put it in as Minerva."

"Do you want me to call you Minerva too?"

"I want you to call me Minnie. But I want you to think of me as Minerva."

"Why?"

"It's what I want. Just because. I don't have a real reason. Do I need one?"

"But—"

"Sweet dreams, David Salmon."

"Good night, Minnie Drugas."

After the last text, I put down the phone on the nightstand next to my bed and stared at the screen. For half a minute, I sat on the edge of my bed and stared at it. I felt like it had done something sneaky to me. The low battery light was glowing red in the right corner, but I decided not to charge it that night. I didn't want it watching me while I slept. I lay down in bed and pulled the covers up. Then I glanced over at the phone again. The screen had gone dark. I took three deep breaths. I rolled over, reached onto the nightstand, and plugged in the phone.

"Did you make any progress?" I asked Winston on Wednesday morning. He was sitting on the stoop of my house, and I almost hit him in the back when I pushed open the front door. He hopped up and glared at me, like I should have been more careful.

Then, a second later, his look got softer. "Your old man still asleep?"

"How did you know?"

"You weren't hollering to him as you came out the door, were you?"

"I left him a note on the kitchen table," I said.

"Now there's a good boy," Winston said. "Well done, you."

"He's having a hard time. You shouldn't make fun of him."

He put his forearm over his eyes, as if he were ashamed.

"You still haven't answered my question," I said, as we started to walk.

"What question would that be, young squire?"

"Did you make any progress?"

"Toward what?"

"Did you figure out whatever it is we're supposed to be doing together?"

"Not a lick of it," he said.

"How long do you think it's going to take?"

"You want a rough estimate or an exactly-precisely number of days?"

"Either one would be nice," I said.

"What if I said it's going to take as long as it takes?"

I grinned at him. "I'd think you were ducking the question."

He put his hands together and raised them to his chest, like he was praying. "Don't put me under the hot lights, sir!"

"Suppose you're a demon...."

"Oh, I *do* like the sound of that!"

"How do I know, if you're a demon, that you're not making this whole thing up?"

"That's just what a demon *would* do," he said, nodding.

"One the other hand," I said, "if you *are* a demon, there must be a reason you've been sent to bother me, right?"

"Sounds logical."

"What I mean is, demons don't just decide to bother people. They get sent to do it."

"Maybe it's a Jewish thingy," he said.

"Are *you* Jewish?"

"You mean matzos and bitter herbs and all that rubbish? I most certainly am not."

"Don't say it like it's bad."

"Shouldn't you be getting ready for your thirteen thingy?"

"You mean my bar mitzvah?" I asked.

"Chopped liver for your troubles."

"I *told* you. I don't go to Hebrew School. I never have. My mom doesn't believe in it."

"What's she got against it?"

"I don't know," I said. "I don't think she's real high on, you know, religion. It's not a big deal for her. I guess that's how she was raised. It's not like she's dead set against it. It's just not her favorite thing. That's why I never went to Hebrew school."

"How'd that sit with your dad?"

"He went along with my mom."

"So that's who calls the tune…."

"That's not funny," I said.

"No offense meant, guvnor! No offense meant!"

Right then, a car screeched to a stop a half block behind us. We both turned at the same time, as the guy driving the car leaned on his horn. That was when I noticed Minnie running across the street toward us. She was ignoring the driver, and a second later, he gave up honking at her and drove away.

I stared at her in amazement.

"Caught you!" she called, slightly out of breath. "I knew it."

"That car almost hit you!"

She smiled. "Except it didn't, and don't change the subject."

"What are you talking about?"

"I caught you!" she repeated.

"You caught me?"

"I caught you talking to yourself."

I glanced over my shoulder. Winston was gone.

"You almost got killed!"

"*Except I didn't,*" she said, then rolled her eyes.

"Wait…don't you live in the other direction?"

"Hector told me you'd be walking along Jewel Avenue, so I came looking for you."

"Why didn't you'd wait at the fire hydrant?"

"Because I wanted to see you first, before you got to the fire hydrant. Except I didn't know which side of the street you'd be on."

I gave her a weird look, and she gave me a weird look back.

Then we started to walk toward Talbot.

"Can I ask you a personal question?" she said.

"If you want."

"No, but it's a *real* personal question."

"I already said all right."

"Do you ever get mad at your mom?"

"Why would I get mad at my mom?"

"You know why."

"She wasn't happy with her life," I said. "She made a choice. You can't get mad at her for that."

"Yeah, but she must have known she was going to hurt you."

"I'm sure she did. I'm sure she knew it was going to hurt both of us, me and my dad. But that tells you how bad she wanted out. It's not like she was *trying* to hurt anybody."

"Did she and your dad argue a lot?"

"I wouldn't say *a lot*. But, sure, they argued. That's a natural thing. But they weren't arguing more than usual. If you're going to ask me whether I saw it coming, the answer is no, definitely not."

"You just sound so casual about it," she said.

"What can you do?"

"That's what I mean!"

"But there's nothing you *can* do," I said.

"Except cry and cry."

"Is that what you did after your parents got divorced?"

"For like nine months, that was pretty much *all* I did."

"Why did they get divorced?"

"My dad cheated on my mom," Minnie said. "He cheated *a lot*. It got to the point where my mom couldn't take it anymore, so they had this huge fight, and a few weeks later she and I moved out."

"He cheated a lot?"

"*A lot*."

"Like how much?"

"He probably had twenty-five girlfriends."

"C'mon!"

"Maybe more."

"At the same time?" I asked.

That cracked her up. "No, not at the same time. He might've had two or three at the same time though."

"Is he like a rock star?"

"Close," she said. "He's a concert promoter. He works with lots of famous musicians. He's the guy who sets things up, who takes care of them, who makes their arrangements, you know, like where they play and where they stay. He has eleven people working for him. Nine of them are women."

"Why are so many of them women?"

"Think about it, David."

"Oh."

"Bingo," she said. "He calls me every week, like nothing ever happened, like he wants to bond. But all we talk about is what concerts he's working on, never anything that matters. It's pathetic! I keep a log of his clients since that's what I used to do when we lived together. He paid me to do it. That was my allowance. So as long as I keep the log going, he gets to pretend things are still the same between us."

"Why do you keep doing it?"

"Because he still sends me money. But it's just a lie. It's just a stupid, stupid lie."

"My dad owns a dry cleaners."

"He's probably pretty different than my dad."

"You and I are probably pretty different too."

"Probably," she said. "But opposites attract."

She gave me another weird look.

I noticed it, but I kept walking.

Minnie and I walked the three blocks to the fire hydrant together, where we met up with Hector. The look on his face when he saw us coming was a mixture of *You've got to be kidding*! and *Oh, gross*! But he nodded his usual hello. He didn't say anything to make the situation more awkward.

After Minnie headed off to her homeroom, Hector poked his elbow in my side. "You like her, don't you?"

"She's all right," I said.

"But you *like* her."

"Sure, I like her. Don't you like her?"

"Yes, I like her. But I don't *like* her."

I shook my head. "Let it go, okay?"

"I'm not criticizing you. I'm glad."

As we got to homeroom, Hector veered off toward his desk in the back, and I headed to mine at the far end of the second row. But when I glanced up, Winston was sitting at my desk, smiling up at me. I walked over to the desk, stopped, and stared down at him—what else could I do? Then I gestured with my head for him to get up. That made him smile even more.

Without moving my lips, as low as I could, I whispered, "You can't be here."

"And yet here I am."

"I have to sit down."

"There are plenty of other seats for your arse, mate. You snooze, you lose...."

"You're going to get me in trouble."

Mrs. Pang walked through the classroom door at that moment. I glanced over my left shoulder at her, and when I turned back, Winston was gone. I slid down into my seat and took out the notebook from my backpack. Mrs. Pang began her morning's announcements, and I took a deep breath.

Hector and I were sitting in the cafeteria during lunch period, picking at what was left of our eggplant rollatini, when one of the security guys walked over to our table. He was a round-shouldered guy with a big sandbag-shaped face, and he needed a shave. I could feel Hector tense up through the bench. How could you blame him? The security guys left you alone unless there was a problem.

The guy said, "Which one of you two is Salmon?"

"That's me."

"You know where Mr. Ivan's office is?"

"Yeah."

"You need me to walk you there?"

"No," I said.

"What about me?" Hector asked.

"You're good."

The security guy walked me as far as the cafeteria exit, then pointed in the direction of Mr. Ivan's office and nodded. "No detours, got it?"

"Got it."

Mr. Ivan was standing outside his office, waiting for me. He waved me inside, and I sat down on the couch.

"How are things going?" Mr. Ivan asked.

"You mean since yesterday?"

"Yes, I wanted to follow up on our visit."

"I took more notes in history. I'm sure I'll do better on the next quiz."

"I'm pleased to hear that," he said. "What about your other classes?"

"I'm doing fine in those."

"What about homeroom?"

"What do you mean?"

"Are you doing well in your homeroom?"

"There's no work in homeroom," I said. "It's just announcements."

"I'm aware of that. Are you getting along with the other students?"

"Yes…"

"Do you mind if I cut to the chase, David?"

"I don't mind."

"I received a report about you this morning from Mrs. Pang, and I was concerned by it. Do you know what I'm referring to? Take a moment and think hard before you answer that question."

I thought hard. "No, I honestly don't know what you're referring to."

"Several of your classmates heard you talking to yourself," he said.

I felt my face get hot. "Oh, *that*."

"Are you hearing voices, David?"

I forced a laugh. "No, it's dumb."

"You can be honest with me. You haven't done anything wrong."

"It's nothing like that."

"Then what is it?" Mr. Ivan asked.

"I just...I just sometimes think out loud. But if it's freaking people out, I—"

"I'm not worried about other people's reactions. I'm worried about you."

"I guess I've been doing it more lately," I said. "I'll definitely stop though."

"David, you've had a shock to your system."

"I know I have—"

"And I realize you're sad about it. It's only natural that it's a distraction."

"Except it isn't," I said. "I know I messed up that quiz, but I'll do better."

"I have to do my job, David. Will you let me do my job?"

"Sure."

"On a scale of one to ten, ten being the worst, how sad are you right now?"

It seemed like a dumb question, but I took a second to think it over; I knew Mr. Ivan was only doing his job, and I really and truly wanted to help him out. "I guess it would be a four."

"Only a four?"

"Yeah," I said.

"Would you say that your four is more likely to change into a five or into a three?"

"I don't know. It feels like a pretty solid four right now."

Mr. Ivan smiled at me. "Sounds like a truthful answer."

"It *is* a truthful answer."

He stood up, walked over to the door, and held it open. "You have about ten minutes left before the period bell. I'm sorry I dragged you away from your lunch."

"That's all right," I said. "I was done anyway."

Winston was leaning against the wall across from Mr. Ivan's office. His arms were folded over his chest, and he was tapping his foot in a comical way, the way a guy taps his foot when he wants you to know he's been waiting for a long time.

"As I live and breathe!" he said.

I walked right past him. I didn't say a word. I didn't even slow down.

"Don't be like that, boy!"

I didn't look back. I just kept walking in the direction of the cafeteria.

He followed me. "The silent treatment, is it? You think that'll work?"

I shrugged and kept walking.

I heard him stop. He shouted, "I've been married, you know…twice!"

I waved him off with the back of my right hand but didn't answer.

His voice got more desperate. "I can take whatever you dish out!"

The security guy noticed me come back into the cafeteria. We made eye contact, and I nodded at him. He nodded back; I wasn't sure whether it was a friendly nod, or he meant that he had his eye on me. Hector was still sitting at our table in the cafeteria, still picking at his rollatini.

He didn't see me until I slid in next to him; then he smiled.

"What was that about?" he said.

"Mrs. Pang told Mr. Ivan that I was talking to myself this morning."

Hector started to laugh. "You always do that."

"That's what I told Mr. Ivan."

"Did you get in trouble?"

"No, not really. But if you catch me doing it, let me know, all right?"

Right then, Minnie strolled over and sat down across from us. "Hi."

"Don't you have lunch next period?" I asked.

"How did you know? Have you been doing some investigating?"

"No!"

"That's all right if you have," she said. "I've got nothing to hide."

"Did you cut out of class?" Hector asked.

"I did no such thing! I told my art teacher I was feeling weak, and she said I could get lunch a few minutes early. So here I am."

"Were you feeling weak?" I asked.

"Maybe," Minnie said. "But the question is *why* I was feeling weak. Do you mind if I eat with you guys?"

Hector said, "We don't mind, but we're going to have to clear out in like a minute."

Just then, the bell sounded.

Minnie looked at me, mournfully. "*Que lastima...*"

"What does that mean?" I asked.

Hector laughed. "It means *what a pity*. But that's not how you pronounce it."

Minnie stuck out her tongue. "That's as far as we've gotten in Spanish One."

On my walk home after school, I got about three blocks from Talbot before Winston showed up. He was standing at a mailbox, acting like he'd just dropped in a letter, jiggling the handle.

He turned as I got close to him and shouted, "David Salmon! As I live and breathe!"

I walked right passed him…again.

"C'mon, Davey boy! Don't be like that!"

I ignored him and kept going.

"All right, I apologize," he said.

I didn't slow down but called back, "What are you apologizing for?"

"I was out of line showing up in your classroom the way I did," he said. "I thought it would be a giggle, and maybe it would've been a giggle somewhere else, but I did what I did, and it was wrong, and now it's all this."

I stopped and turned around. "You got me in trouble."

"Did I?"

"You *almost* did."

"How can I make it up to you, mate?"

"We've got to have rules," I said.

"What kind of rules?"

"No more showing up at school."

"Done!"

"That means nowhere *near* school either. Like where we are now, that's as close as you can come to Talbot. Three blocks away. Do we have a deal or not?"

"Deal."

He put out his hand, and I shook it, and we started to walk again.

"I hear you've got a bird," he said.

"What? I don't have a bird."

"No, I mean a *bird*…a girlfriend."

"You mean Minnie? C'mon, I only met her yesterday."

"True enough, but women know things faster than us menfolk do."

"You were married twice?"

"Who told you that?" he said.

"You did…in the hallway…when I wouldn't talk to you."

"Ah, yes."

"Did you get a divorce?"

"Yes, I did."

"Why?"

"You know how it is," he said. "I used to be cruel."

I glanced up to read the expression on his face. You could tell it wasn't a subject he liked to talk about, so I let it drop.

"Anyway, I'm curious about something," I said.

That perked him up. "Sign of an intellectual!"

"When you're not with me, where do you go?"

"Excellent question! Top notch!"

"What's the answer?"

"Haven't got a clue."

"How can that be?"

"I don't remember," he said. "Clearly, I must be somewhere, but it feels like nowhere. You know what I mean? It's like I go blank. Like I blackout or something. Then, the next thing I know, I open my eyes, and I'm with you. It's a proper phenomenon is what it is."

"You don't visit anybody else?" I asked.

"Not that I can remember."

"You don't remember anything else?"

"Not a thing."

"That means you don't understand what's going on any more than I do."

"That's the long and the short of it," he said.

"But you know there's something we're supposed to do together?"

"Yes."

"Something we're supposed to set right?"

"I know it sounds wobbly, but yeah, that's the nub of the gist."

"*Do* you know how it sounds?" I asked. "Because 'wobbly' isn't the word."

"What is the word, Davey. Say the word."

"Crazy," I said. "Crazy is the word. The whole thing sounds crazy."

"Could be we're a pair, my boy. Could be we're a regular pair."

Might as Well be Dead

The phone woke me up on Thursday morning. It was on the edge of the nightstand, about six inches from my face. I had it set on vibrate, but when it vibrated, it rattled against the wood surface, and when it rattled, it started to teeter; I grabbed it before it fell on the floor.

I rubbed the sleep out of my eyes with my forearm and mumbled, "Hello?"

I realized, even before my eyes focused, it was my mom. "Hello, David."

"What time is it?" I moaned.

"Did I wake you up?"

"Yes."

"I should have let you sleep."

"No, it's okay. I don't mind."

"Your voice sounds strange."

"It's because I just woke up."

"No, that's not it," she said. "It's something else."

"I don't know…"

"Like you've grown up all of a sudden."

I yawned into the phone. "There's this girl—"

"Oh no!" She started to laugh.

"Please don't make a big deal out of it, Mom."

"But it *is* a big deal. You have a girlfriend…."

"It's not like it's official or anything," I said. "Her name is Minerva"

"Minerva?"

"But everyone calls her Minnie."

"Oh, David! I'm going to cry!"

A second later, she was weeping into the phone.

"C'mon, don't do that. Why are you crying?"

"Because I'm missing it!" she sobbed. "Because I want to meet her! Because I want to see the two of you together!"

"Well..."

Her voice got stiff. "David, you know I can't come back. That wouldn't be fair to your father, and it wouldn't be fair to you either. It's not the kind of thing you can go back and forth with."

"I know," I said.

"You know I'm thinking about you all the time, every hour of every day. That's never going to change."

"I know."

"But I also have a new life now, and I've got to get on with it."

"I know."

"That doesn't mean I don't want to know *everything*," she said. "Do you swear to tell me *everything* about you and your Minnie?"

"Well, not *everything*."

She started to laugh again. "Don't tell me you're keeping secrets from your mother!"

That made me laugh. "I guess maybe I am."

I rolled over and tried to go back to sleep, but a couple of minutes later, the phone went off again. This time it was a text message. It was from Hector: "I need to talk to you about something, okay?"

"Okay," I texted back.

I pushed back the covers and sat up on the edge of the bed, expecting another text. But none came. I waited for three minutes, but he didn't text me back. I got fed up and wrote, "Well?"

"I don't want to text back and forth," he wrote. "I want to talk."

"Okay."

I squinted at the phone. That felt like the end of the conversation.

"Are you mad at me?" I texted him. "Did I do something wrong?"

"No, it's nothing like that." He attached three yellow smile emojis.

I put down the phone and headed to the bathroom to wash my face. The warm water felt good, so I washed my face twice, then cupped my hands and drank several handfuls of water, which tasted like soap. I spit the last handful into the sink, then dried my face and went back to my room.

Winston was leaning back in the desk chair with his feet on the edge of my bed. He yawned in a comical way. "Keep an eye on young Mr. Salmon," he said. "He's an early riser. Mark my words, he's going to get that worm."

"You've got your shoes on my blanket."

"Which is a problem, why?"

"Because your shoes are dirty."

"True enough, but I'm not real," he said. "Hence, *ipso facto quod erat demonstrandum cogito ergo sum* the dirt on my shoes must not be real either."

Before I could answer him, there was a knock at the door. "David, you decent?"

I turned to the door, then turned back to Winston... and, as usual, he was gone.

"Yeah, I'm decent, Dad."

He pushed open the door. He was wearing his plaid bathrobe and brown slippers.

"You got a minute?"

"Sure," I said.

He sat down on my desk chair, and it creaked under his weight. I sat down at the edge of my bed, right where Winston had rested his feet. My dad focused his eyes on mine. "How do you feel?"

"All right."

"You sure you're all right?"

"Yeah, I'm sure."

"You'd let me know if something was wrong, right?"

"Yeah."

"I'm going to level with you, David. I got a call at work yesterday from a counselor at your school. He said his name was Ivan. You know who that is?"

"Yeah," I said.

"He thinks you're, you know, not doing so hot."

"That's his opinion."

"He said that maybe I should get you to see a therapist. What do you think about that?"

"I don't need to see a therapist!"

"He said you were talking to yourself."

"C'mon!"

"David, I just heard you talking to yourself...through the door...a minute ago."

I closed my eyes, took a deep breath, then opened them again. "What if I am?"

"That means you're not doing so hot," he said.
"Don't you ever talk to yourself?"
"I'm an adult, David. It's a different situation."
"What if I told you I've got an imaginary friend, an English guy, or maybe Australian, I'm not sure which, who shows up out of nowhere, and we have long talks about stuff?"

That cracked him up, but not for long. "I'm trying to have a serious conversation with you."

"I know you are, Dad. But it's not—"

"You got to help me out here. I don't know what to do. You're *talking to yourself—*"

"So you're saying it's a problem if I'm talking to myself, but it's not a problem if I'm talking to an imaginary English guy?"

"Is he telling you to do things?"

I shook my head. "Not so far."

"You're pulling my leg, right?"

I nodded. "I'm fine, Dad. I'm really and truly fine."

He stood up and patted the top of my head. But I think he realized it was a dumb thing to be doing, like I was *way* too old for him to be patting me on the head, so he messed my hair with his fingers and pretended that that was what he meant to do all along. Then he shuffled out of the room.

I got up from the bed and pushed the desk chair back under the desk.

Winston was sitting on the edge of the bed when I turned back around. He smiled and flashed me a quick okay sign, and I rolled my eyes.

Might as Well be Dead

Hector was waiting for me at the fire hydrant, but Minnie wasn't with him. He was half-sitting, half-leaning on the hydrant, with his arms folded across his chest; it made him look posed and awkward, which was how I felt as I walked up to him. For a few seconds, neither of us spoke. We kind of avoided eye contact. Then, when I couldn't take it anymore, I said, "Well?"

"Well, what?"

"You texted me that you needed to talk about something."

"Oh *that*," he said. "Yeah, well, it turned out to be nothing."

"What do you mean it turned out to be nothing?"

"It's not important. Or it's not as important as I thought."

"What is *it*?" I asked.

"Nothing. Let it go."

"Is it something to do with Minnie?"

"What? No, it's nothing like that."

"C'mon, you've got me curious!"

"I'll tell you eventually. But right now, it's not important."

"Hector…"

His slapped his forehead with his palm. "No, David!"

"Then just—"

"End of discussion!"

The rest of the morning, as we went from class to class, Hector froze me out, like *I'd* done something to *him*. But by lunch, he was back to his normal self. I was still curious, but I didn't want to hit another iceberg, so I let the thing, whatever it was, drop.

He'd tell me when he felt like telling me.

During lunch, Mr. Ivan showed up in the cafeteria. It was the first time I'd ever seen him there, and for a second I thought he was going to come over and sit down at our table. But he strolled past us and into the kitchen. When he came out, he was sipping a carton of milk through a straw. This time, though, he glanced over at our table and winked at me.

Hector noticed the wink.

"What was that about?"

"He called my dad yesterday," I said.

"About what?"

"He thinks I should see a therapist."

"Why? Well, I know why. But *why*?"

"I guess he thinks I'm a little crazy."

"*Are* you a little crazy?"

"Oh, for sure," I said. "Want to see my ear wax models?"

"It's not so bad, you know."

"What isn't so bad?"

"Therapy," he said.

"I'm sure it's great…if you're making ear wax models."

"I was in therapy," he said.

"Really?"

"Yes."

"Is that what you wanted to tell me—"

"No, it's not…and *let's move on*."

"Why were you in therapy?" I asked.

"I was feeling stressed out last year."

"You never told me."

Hector smiled. "You never asked me."

"Are you still doing it?"

"You mean going to therapy? No, I stopped after six months."

"Did you get cured?"

"That's not how it works, David. You don't get cured."

"Then what's the point?"

"You feel better, and you understand yourself better."

"What if I feel okay, and I understand myself okay?"

"Then you probably don't need therapy," Hector said.

I thought for sure Minnie would meet up with us after school let out, that she'd rush out of her last class and find us, but Hector and I walked down to the fire hydrant and went our separate ways with no sign of her. No sign of Winston either, which meant that he was sticking to our deal. But as I turned up Jewel Avenue and walked another few blocks, as weird as it sounds, I felt kind of lonely.

That was when I got a text from Minnie. "Did you talk to Hector?"

"About what?" I wrote back.

"I knew he'd chicken out!"

"Do you know what he wanted to talk to me about?"

Half a minute passed before I got her answer. "No."

"Obviously, you know."

"Even if I do, it's not my place to say," she wrote.

"If you know, then I have a right to know too."

"Says who?"

"I'm Hector's best friend," I wrote back, "and he's my best friend."

She began to answer, the message dots were rolling, but stopped.

Another half a minute passed; I was staring hard at the phone.

"What if you come over on Saturday, and I cook pralines for us?"

"If I come over," I wrote, "will you tell me what Hector told you?"

"Maybe."

"What's your address?"

She texted me her address.

"What time do you want me to get there?"

"Noon."

I started to write, "It's a date." But I caught myself and deleted "It's a d—"

Instead, I wrote, "I'll be there at noon."

About a second later, Minnie wrote back, "So it's a date, right?"

"Yes."

"Should I pretend nothing is going on tomorrow?"

"What do you mean?"

"Tomorrow, at school. Should I pretend we don't have a date on Saturday?"

"I don't care," I wrote.

"Guys sometimes like to pretend about that kind of stuff. I think it's dumb."

"You don't have to pretend. I really don't care."

"Don't say it like THAT! It sounds like you don't care that we have a date."

"That's not what I meant."

"Good, then I'll see you tomorrow, and again on Saturday for our DATE."

That ended the conversation.

"You're a heartbreaker, young Mister!"

I turned around, and Winston was looking over my shoulder at the phone.

"Lay off!" I said.

"Be wary, squire."

"Wary of what?"

"You can shine your shoes and wear a suit."

"Why would I do that?"

"You can comb your hair and look quite cute."

"Did you just make that up? What does it have to do with anything?"

"It's sound advice," he said. "Get your feet back on the ground first."

"Meaning?"

"Proceed with caution."

"All right, I get it," I said. "Why didn't you say that in the first place?"

"Style, my boy! Style!"

The sight of my mom's stuff still scattered in boxes around the living room got me mad. My dad had rearranged the boxes at least three times in the last week, stacked them in different ways, pushed one stack to the corner and another to the center of the floor and left one box open for more stuff. Basically, he'd done nothing.

He was worried about *me*?

The rocking chair creaked, and a shiver went down my spine; Winston was sitting in it, rocking back and forth.

"So do you have any thirty-three-and-a-thirds?"

"What's that?"

"Vinyl," he said. "Do you keep any in the house?"

"I don't know what you're talking about," I said.

"*Records*!"

"My dad has some CDs upstairs…."

He turned up his nose. "Never touch the stuff. What about those two boxes right over there?"

"Those are my mom's."

He bounded out of the rocking chair and pounced on the boxes. Then he began to sniff at them. "I smell the Rolling Stones."

"C'mon, they're taped up."

"Then get me the scissors, boy! Off you go, and don't forget to run back with them…."

"I'm not opening my mom's record boxes," I said. "Do you know how long it took my dad to pack them?"

"Fess up, Davey! I know you're a musical. I've seen you walking about with those ear-plug thingies."

"Well, sure, I like music."

"What kind?" he asked.

"I like rap."

"*Really?* Nice Hebrew fellow like yourself?"
"Do you have something against Jewish people?"
"Not in the least. Some of my best accountants…"
"Stop it!"
He pushed his glasses down his nose and smiled. "You're not going to report me, are you?"
"Report you to who? You're not even real."
He cleared his throat. "To return to the topic, what if we just open one wee box?"
"No!"
"Who's your mom's favorite?"
"The Beatles," I said.
"You don't say!"
"Do you like the Beatles?"
Winston thought it over. "Never heard of them."
"C'mon!"
"What's so special about them?"
"My mom used to make me listen to them when I was little."
"Couldn't she have paddled your bottom like a regular mom?"
That cracked me up. "No, you don't get it. The Beatles were her 'holy of holies.' That's what she called them. She'd say, 'Are you ready for the holy of holies?' Then she'd pull out a Beatles record and play it. I haven't thought about that in a long time. It's funny how you remember things. I guess she misses them a lot…which is why there's no way I'm opening her record boxes. It's like a miracle my dad ever got them packed up."
"What about you?" Winston asked. "Do you like old timey songs?"

"You mean like Maroon 5?"

"I mean like stuff that I'd like," he said.

"I like that song 'Rolling on the River.'"

"Now you're talking!"

He started to clap his hands in rhythm. I only stared at him at first, but he kept going until I clapped too. Then he started to sing. He messed up some of the words; I wasn't sure of them myself, but at one point he sang "pumped a lot of plates," which makes no sense. But he had a real good voice, like a *professional* voice; it was friendly and sarcastic and sweet and rough at the same time. I wanted to sing along with him but didn't; I only kept clapping since I wanted to listen to his voice.

When he got to the end of the song, I applauded, and I meant it.

He took a long, deep bow.

Friday was a nothing sort of day. The most interesting thing that happened at school was that I got a seventy on my history quiz. That might not sound like much, but it was good enough to get Mr. Ivan off my case. Really, I should have gotten a seventy-five. I had to finish the quotation, "We hold these truths to be ____" The right answer is "self-evident." I wrote "obvious," which is technically wrong, but it means the same thing…which, in my opinion, should be worth half credit. But a seventy meant I'd passed, and Mr. Ivan gave me a quick thumbs-up as we crossed paths in the hall before lunch. Of course, that thumbs-up also meant he was still talking to my teachers, keeping track of how I was doing. It annoyed me, thinking about it. But what could I do? That's how things were going to be for a while. It wasn't Mr. Ivan's fault. It wasn't even Winston's fault, even though talking to him was what got me in hot water. It was my own fault for being careless.

Hector seemed more relieved than I was when I showed him the history quiz.

"You studied, didn't you?"

"Yeah, a little bit," I said.

"It makes a difference."

"Who said it didn't?"

"What are you planning to bring to Minnie's house tomorrow?"

"She told you?" I asked.

"We walk to school together every morning. What do *you* think?"

"Am I supposed to bring something?"

"Yes," he said, and he sounded sure.

"All right, what should I bring?"

"Flowers," he said. "For her mom."

"What about for Minnie?"

"You don't have to bring a present for Minnie. You can bring one if you feel like it, but it's not necessary. You're her present. That's how you should think about it. But definitely bring flowers for her mom. Trust me. That's how it works."

"How do you know? Do you have a girlfriend you haven't told me about?"

He shook his head, but he had a weird look on his face.

"*Do* you have a girlfriend?" I asked. "Is that what you were going to tell me?"

"No!"

"Then how'd you become such an expert?"

He blushed. "Just trust me on this, David."

"Well, then, since you're so smart, where am I supposed to get flowers?"

"There's a flower shop on the corner of our block," Hector said. "If you're riding your bike, you'll pass it before you get to her house. She lives in the third house from the end, the one with the slanted red roof."

"Got it," I said.

"Oh, and don't be surprised if she avoids you for the rest of today."

"Why? Is she mad at me?"

"No," Hector said, smiling. "It's nothing like that. She got what she wants. The two of you have a date. Why would she give you a chance to change your mind?"

Minnie texted me Saturday morning to make sure I'd get to her house around noon. There wasn't much back and forth. I texted back that I'd be there. She sent me a thumbs-up sign. That was it.

The ride out to Minnie's house took a half hour. I already knew the way because she lived down the block from Hector, and I'd ridden my bike to his house lots of times. I could have done it in less than a half hour, maybe twenty minutes, since the wind was behind me, but I took my time; I coasted entire blocks without pedaling. I was about halfway when a red bike pulled up alongside me. Winston was riding it, wearing an orange helmet that was like three sizes too big for his head, smiling sarcastically. He had rubber bands around his pant cuffs, and he wasn't wearing socks, so you could see his bare ankles. The bike itself was making a loud, rattling noise, like the wheels were about to fly off any second.

"Careful there, Vicar!" he called.

"Sweet ride."

"You like it, then?"

"Yeah, it's very…red."

"I rented it at the Make-Believe Bicycle Shop."

"You know you can't come to Minnie's house."

"Figured as much," he said.

"But you can ride along for a while if you want."

"Want to hear my ringy-dingy thingy?"

He rang the little metal bell on his left handlebar.

"I guess I'm the only one who can hear it," I said.

"Just you and that wolf-in-sheep's-clothing…."

I glanced over my right shoulder and saw a collie galloping across the front lawn of a house. The dog rushed to the edge of the yard until it came to a brown picket fence. Then, at once, it started to bark. There was no question it was barking at us, at the sound of Winston's bell. He rang it again, and the bark got even louder.

The dog was still barking as we rode out of earshot.

"How is that possible?" I asked.

"My theory is that the dog can read your mind."

"That's just stupid!"

"I said it was a theory. I didn't say it was true."

"No, seriously. What *are* you?"

"That again!"

"It's bugging me," I said.

"Driving you nuts, is it?"

"I'm *not* nuts!"

"But you've got a screw loose. You said as much yourself."

"There's a difference between crazy and nuts," I said.

"If you say so."

"Stop changing the subject! What are you?"

"Like I told you last time, I'm working on it."

"Are you at least making progress?" I asked.

"Maybe a bit, I think."

"What have you got?"

"I *think*—and mind you, it's only a thought at the moment—I'm a messenger."

"What kind of messenger?"

"Not sure just yet," he said.

He glanced across at me.

"You look disappointed."

"I'm not disappointed," I said. "But I thought you were more like a *do*er. Like the two of us were going to *do* something. *Set something right*. That was what you said. I didn't think we were going to deliver a message."

"Delivering a message is doing something."

"What's the message?"

"Not sure. But I keep getting…I don't know what you'd call 'em. *Inklings*, maybe."

"Wait a minute. Is the message for me?"

He stopped pedaling and closed his eyes real tight. He coasted for several seconds like that, with his eyes closed. Then he opened his eyes again.

"Sorry, it's no good," he said. "But it's right there, right on the tip of me noggin. Not to worry. I'll get it figured out sooner or later."

I stopped at the flower shop on the corner of Minnie's block and bought a bunch of flowers for Minnie's mom, like Hector suggested. Minnie lived in the right half of a red brick house. The two front doors were right next to one another. There was a three-step stoop that led up to the doors. She was out front, sitting at the top of the stoop, as I rolled into her driveway. She jumped up as soon as she saw me and lunged forward a few steps, but then she looked back toward the window over her left shoulder and stopped. She gave me a casual wave and waited for me to get off my bike and come to her.

I pushed the bike up the driveway, kicked down the kickstand, and pushed it onto the lawn at the edge of the garage door. It felt awkward, the way she was watching me the entire time but not moving; it made me self-conscious about every move.

Afterward, when I walked up to her, she kissed me on both cheeks.

"You got me flowers?" she said.

"They're for your mom."

"She's watching us," she whispered into my ear. "Don't look!"

Might as Well be Dead

I looked straight at Minnie's eyes. "Why is she watching us?"

"To make sure I act like a lady."

I caught myself before I laughed out loud.

"It's not funny!" she whispered.

She locked her right arm through my left arm and led me to her front door. It swung open before we got there, and her mom was smiling down at us as we walked up the three brick steps, arm in arm.

"Minerva, you didn't tell me David was so handsome!" she said. "Welcome to our humble abode!"

I handed her the flowers as I walked up the steps.

"What a gentleman you are!" she said.

Minnie's mom was short. That was the first thing I noticed about her. She was *maybe* five feet tall and real thin. She had dark brown eyes, light brown hair that came down past her shoulders, and a long narrow nose that hooked slightly downward. But it was her height that stood out because it meant I could look her in the eyes as soon as I got to the top of the stoop.

She kissed me on both cheeks, the same way Minnie had. Then she stepped back and put her hands on her hips. Before I knew it, she'd put down the flowers and taken out her phone, and she was snapping pictures of me and Minnie standing next to one another, with our arms still locked together.

After that, the two of them gave me a tour of their house. Mrs. Drugas called it "the grand tour," except she said it in a sarcastic way since it wasn't a big house. Downstairs were the kitchen, living room, and bathroom, and upstairs were two bedrooms, a couple of closets, and that was pretty much it.

"It's a lot like my house," I said.

Minnie squeezed my arm. "I can't wait to see your house!"

We wound up back in the kitchen, where Mrs. Drugas had laid out all the ingredients to make pralines. The thing that caught my attention was a stick of butter; it had started to go soft. Butter wasn't my favorite thing to begin with, and the sight of butter-sweat running down the sides grossed me out. The rest of the ingredients weren't so bad. Hazelnuts. Milk. White and brown sugar.

"Do you want to help or just watch?" Minnie asked.

"Just watch," I said.

"Wonderful!" Mrs. Drugas said. "Then you and I can get to know one another while Minerva does all the work!"

Suddenly, the butter wasn't looking as gross....

But Mrs. Drugas turned out to be all right. Mostly, she kept me updated about what Minnie was doing, like a baseball announcer. "Now she's going to add a cup of hazelnuts to the pot...and now she's stirring in the sugars...and now a drop of vanilla...." She also called out a couple of things to Minnie in Greek, and Minnie nodded back at her.

Toward the end, though, she started to ask me personal questions, like about how my dad and I were doing with my mom gone. It bugged me, but I didn't let on. I smiled and told her how our living room was still cluttered with boxes of my mom's stuff, and how my dad was having a hard time shipping it out. Then, out of nowhere, she said that maybe she'd give my dad a call, if that was all right, because she understood how hard it was to let go of stuff, and maybe she could help him out. She told me not to worry, that she wouldn't make it too obvious, that she'd tell him she was calling because Minnie and I were friends, so she just wanted to say hello.

But I got the feeling, the more she talked about it, that she wanted to make the call for her own sake, not for my dad's.

After the pralines were cooked and spread out on a baking sheet, Mrs. Drugas left Minnie and me alone in the kitchen. She stepped into the backyard, which you could see through a sliding glass door in the kitchen, sat down in a lawn chair, and started to read a magazine.

"What do you think about my mom?" Minnie said.

"I think she's nice. I didn't know you spoke Greek."

"Oh, I don't speak it. But I understand it. Most of the time, not always."

"I just speak English," I said.

"But what do you *really* think about her? You can be honest, David."

"I am being honest. I think she's nice."

Minnie laughed. "She *is* nice, but she's also lonely since the divorce."

"Oh."

"I think maybe she has a little crush on your dad."

"How could she have a crush on him? She's never even met him."

"Well, I'm *sure* she's googled him," Minnie said. "It's only natural."

"Why is it natural?"

Might as Well be Dead

"Because she wants to know what sort of family you come from."

"I don't see why—"

"Oh, look, I think the pralines have cooled!"

The pralines *were* good. There was no way they were going to be as good as Minnie made them out to be. They weren't the best things in the world, but they were sweet and had a good, chewy texture.

Mrs. Drugas came back inside and put the leftover pralines in the refrigerator. While she was doing that, Minnie led me into the living room and then to the couch. We sat down, and she turned on the TV. For the next hour, she channel-surfed, never staying on the same station for more than a couple of minutes. I didn't mind though. I figured, sooner or later, she was going to bring up Hector; she was going to tell me why Hector wanted to talk to me. That was the deal, the reason I'd come to her house. Maybe, in her mind, I'd come for pralines. And I guess I *had* come for pralines, in a way. But she also said that she would tell me what was going on with Hector.

She changed the channel again and hit on a retro music video show, so I asked her to turn up the volume. I scooted closer to her on the coach and said in a low voice, "What does Hector want to talk to me about?"

"Oh, *that*."

"Yeah, that. What's his deal?"

"Don't ask me that, David…."

"Why not?"

"I don't feel right telling you," she said. "I mean, how would you feel if the shoe was on the other foot?"

"I don't know how I'd feel since I don't know what kind of shoe we're talking about."

"You're putting me in a difficult position." She scrunched her shoulders, then turned and looked straight at me. "You're my sweetheart, but Hector's my friend. You're making me choose."

"But you *said* you'd tell me."

"I said *maybe* I'd tell you."

"C'mon, that's not right."

"Maybe means maybe."

I took a deep breath and stood up. "If you say so."

"Where are you going?"

"I'm going home," I said.

"Why?"

"Because maybe means maybe."

"It *does*...."

"But you knew what I thought," I said.

She grabbed my hand and pulled me back down onto the couch. She gave me a long, serious look. "If I tell you, you have to swear you'll never tell Hector I told you. I mean it, you have to *swear*. You have to say the words, 'I swear I'll never tell Hector.' Or else I'm not going to tell you."

"I swear I'll never tell Hector," I said.

"Now you have to kiss me...on the lips."

"Why do I—"

"It's a real swear. The kiss makes it official."

I leaned forward and kissed her on the lips.

She smiled. "That was our first official kiss."

"I guess."

"That's all you have to say? *You guess?*"

"It was a good kiss," I said.

"Why is it so hard for you to say something nice? It's like pulling teeth!"

"I liked the kiss. Really and truly, I did."

"You're not just saying that?"

"No, I'm not just saying that. I really and truly want to kiss you again."

"You can," she said. "Whenever you want, as long as you ask me first."

"How can I kiss you again until I know what Hector wants to talk to me about?"

"What does one thing have to do with the other?"

"It's a distraction," I said. "I can't concentrate."

Minnie put her hand on the back of my neck and pulled our faces close together. For a second, I thought she was going to kiss me again, but her eyes got wide, and she whispered, "Hector likes boys."

I leaned back. "What?"

"He likes boys…he's gay."

"He told you that?"

"Yes."

"Why would he tell you that?"

"Because he's gay," she said.

"No, why would he tell *you* that? Why wouldn't he tell me?"

"I don't know."

"It makes no sense. I'm his best friend."

"Maybe that's the reason," Minnie said.

"How can that be the reason?"

"*You're his best friend.* He's got more to lose if he tells you."

"What does he have to lose?" I said.

"Think about it for a minute."

"What? He thinks I won't be his friend because he's gay?"

"It's possible."

"But that's—"

"I'm not saying it's true," she said. "I'm saying it's possible."

"But it's dumb. How could he think that? It's like an insult."

"I'm sure he'll tell you."

"I have to talk to him—"

"No!"

"But how can I—"

"You swore!" she said.

"But that was before I knew—"

"You swore, and I trusted you!"

She started to cry, which caught me off guard. I tried to shush her before her mom heard. When that didn't work, I ran my fingertips through her hair as softly as I could. Her sobbing got quieter as I did that, and a half minute later, she wiped away her tears with her sleeves.

"All right," I said. "I won't talk to Hector until he talks to me."

"You can *talk* to him. Just not about what I told you."

"You know what I mean."

"Oh, and when he does tell you, you have to act surprised."

My neck went slack, and my head hung. "I'll act surprised."

After another hour, Minnie and her mom walked me to the door. Minnie kissed me on both cheeks, like she did when I arrived, and Mrs. Drugas gave me a long hug. Then, a second later, the door shut behind me, and I was standing alone in front of their house. There was a gust of wind, and tree leaves rustled up and down the block. I pushed my bike off the edge of the grass, across the driveway, out into the street, and I hopped on. I took a long, sad look at Hector's house as I rode past it. I wondered whether he was home, whether, maybe, at that moment, he was glancing out of his bedroom window, waiting for me to roll by.

But what could I do?

The ride back felt much longer than the ride to get there. The wind was in my face, and I had to pedal harder than I had in the morning, and even pedaling harder I couldn't work up much speed. For the first half mile, I kept glancing side to side for Winston. He was nowhere in sight. It figured. The one time I wanted him around, you know, to take my mind off stuff, he was a no-show. Meanwhile, I couldn't stop thinking about Hector. How he didn't trust me.

Hector, my best friend, didn't trust me.

That was the part that burned, the fact that he didn't trust me enough to talk to me. Not about stuff that mattered. What did he think was going to happen?

My dad was hunched over, catching his breath, on our front lawn when I got home. He had on a torn blue tee-shirt and a pair of gray gym shorts. He looked up as I rolled onto the driveway. He waved weakly and tried to get out a "hello," but he couldn't come up with enough air.

"What are you doing?" I asked.

He shook his head. "I'm out of shape."

"Were you running?"

"Trying to," he said. "I made it around the block three times."

"That's pretty good."

"Done too much sitting around lately. Needed to stretch my legs. Where have you been?"

"I rode over to Hector's house."

Which wasn't a lie but wasn't *exactly* the truth either.

"He's a good kid," my dad said, then stood up straight. I climbed off the bike and kicked down the kickstand.

"You got plans for next Saturday morning?" he asked.

"Not that I know of."

"How would you feel about going to temple with me?"

"Really?"

"Look," he said, "here's the deal. With everything that's happened, I've been thinking that maybe what we need is a reset. You know, like a new foundation. Something we can build on. You know what I mean? Build ourselves back up."

"But mom never—"

"Well, it's not up to her anymore, is it? I mean, look, here we are. We've got to find our own way. You know?

I was thinking that maybe going to temple could be something to get us going forward."

"Do I *have* to go?"

"No, but I'd appreciate it if you gave the thing a try."

After dinner, I was watching TV in my room. But *watching* is the wrong word; I was looking at it more than watching it. I was sitting in my underwear on my bed, facing the TV screen, and my eyes were open, but if you had asked me what show was on, I wouldn't have been able to tell you. It was like I'd checked out, like my brain had called it a night, except it hadn't bothered to let the rest of me know, so there I was, hunched forward, staring at the TV, and nothing on the screen was getting past my eyeballs.

The thing that snapped me out of it was a text from Hector. "You're going to leave me hanging?"

As weird as it sounds, when I read the message, I wasn't sure whether he'd sent it to me, or I'd zombied-out and sent it to him. For a few seconds, I panicked. My chest got tight, and my heart started to beat fast. What had I done?

I texted back, "What?"

"How did it go?"

"What do you mean?"

"Your date!"

My heart slowed down. "It went fine. Minnie made pralines."

"How were they?"

Might as Well be Dead

"They were fine."
"Just fine?"
"No, they were really good," I wrote. "I liked them."
"Did you meet her mom?"
"Yeah."
"Then I guess you see where Minnie gets it."
"Gets what?"
"Her personality! Are you asleep, David?"
"No."
"Am I bugging you?" he asked.
"No, you're not bugging me."
"It feels like you're not into this."
"Into what?"
"This conversation," he wrote.
"No, it's not that. I'm just tired."
"Why didn't you just say that?"
"I thought you wanted to text."
"I wanted to know how your date went!"
"It went fine."
"Ha ha! I hate you!"
"Really?" I asked.
"Not really. You ARE asleep, aren't you?"
"Oh."
"Get some rest. We can talk on Monday."

Winston was kneeling at the foot of my bed, with his elbows up on the mattress, as I opened my eyes on Sunday morning.

"Are you awake then, Davey boy?"

"Kind of."

"Need a moment to shake off the cobwebs?"

I sat up and slid back against the headboard. "No, I'm awake."

"I picked up a guidebook at the sweet shop around the corner."

"The what?"

"The sweet shop. You know. Magazines, crisps, and the like."

"You mean the candy store?" I asked.

"You have funny names for things over here. But that's the place."

"Why'd you go to the candy store?"

"I told you. I picked up a guidebook. *Things To Do in Flushing.*"

"There's no such book!"

"I've knocked it down to three things to do," he said.

"Which are?"

"How about a baseball game?"

I shook my head. "The season's over."

"Ah."

"Plus, even if it weren't, there's no *way* I'd go to Citi Field with you."

"Probably just as well then. Can't make heads or tails of the sport."

"What else have you got?" I asked.

"Are you saying you're willing to do whatever I say, no matter what?"

"No, I'm saying I've got nothing else to do, so I'm willing to listen."

"The Botanical Gardens. Primrose paths, my boy! Primrose paths!"

I shook my head. "Hay fever."

"Should have guessed as much. The curse of the Semitic proboscis."

"The what?"

"The Jewish nose. The air's free, or so I've been led to believe."

"Keep it up and we won't do anything," I said.

"Sorry. Water under the bridge."

I rolled my eyes. "So what's your third thing?"

He smiled in a sly way. "Flushing Cemetery."

"Is that supposed to be a joke?"

"Less flowers than the Botanical Gardens."

"Yeah, but that's not the point."

"Never know who you'll run into," he said.

"That's gross!"

"C'mon, Davey, it'll be good for a giggle."

"Except it's not funny. It's a cemetery."

"Life is for the living, right?"

"Where did you hear that?"

"Dead guy told me," he said.

I felt a yawn come on, and I used the few seconds to think it over. He seemed to have his heart set on it…and what else did I have to do?

"You really want to go to the cemetery?" I asked.

"Oh, ever so much…"

"All right. Let's go."

"You're a game lad!"

"But don't push it…."

"You're a gentleman and a scholar."

Might as Well be Dead

Flushing Cemetery was either a long walk or a short bike ride from my house; I decided to walk. Riding a bike to a cemetery felt like bad manners, like I was rubbing the fact that I was still alive in the noses of the dead people. Plus, after I got there, I'd have to chain the bike to a street sign, which was a good way to get your front wheel stolen. Walking was definitely the way to go.

The morning was about ten degrees colder than the day before, and a wet wind was swirling in our faces. (I wasn't sure if Winston felt the wind in his face, not being real and all, but I didn't want to start up *that* conversation again.) The air had a definite October feel. Piles of raked leaves were blowing apart and scattering on the front lawns as we walked past them. It was a real pretty walk, at least once you climbed the overpass at 164th Street and cleared the Long Island Expressway. After that, it got scenic. You had St. Mary's on your right, and then Kissena Park on both sides, until you came to Flushing Cemetery.

As we got close, Winston started to whistle. That turned out to be another thing he was good at. I'd heard him whistle before, but more kidding-around, like he was trying to get under my skin. Now, though, he was whistling an entire song. I didn't recognize it, but it sounded calm and sad, and at one point he muttered, "I didn't want to hurt you."

"Who didn't you want to hurt?" I asked.

He looked at me with a confused expression. "What?"

"You said you didn't want to hurt somebody."

"Did I?"

"Yes, you did," I said.

"That's odd because I'm just the sort of rotter who does."

"Who does what?"

"Who hurts people," he answered.

"Why do you say stuff like that?"

"I'm only going by what my friends tell me, Davey."

"Do you have a lot of friends?"

"Millions and millions of 'em."

"C'mon, how can you have *millions* of friends?" I asked.

"You've got to be quick on your feet, let me tell you."

"I don't have a lot of friends."

"You've got that Hector chap," he said.

"I thought I did. Now, I'm not so sure."

"Well, anyway, one good one's enough—in my experience."

"Do you trust your friends?"

"Until they cross me. Then…"

He made a cutting motion across his throat with his thumb.

"You never give them a second chance?"

"Oh, sure. Second chance. Third chance. But after the fifty-seventh chance…"

He made the cutting motion again, then let out a loud laugh.

The black iron gate that stood at the entrance to Flushing Cemetery opened between two brown stone columns. The columns were squared off; they looked like upright coffins topped with concrete beanies. Behind them, as soon as you walked through, there was a mausoleum that looked like it was a thousand years old. That was where dead people were buried above ground, filed away in drawers instead of stuck in the dirt. Winston and I walked past it and headed into the main part of the cemetery. He was walking fast, like he knew right where he was going. I followed three steps behind. He had a funny walk when he was in a rush, with his head tilted forward and his hands folded together against the small of his back.

We made a left turn onto a footpath that ran alongside a narrow road, then walked straight for maybe a hundred yards. Then, all of a sudden, Winston stopped. He stood and stared at a black marble monument. I couldn't make out the name on the monument since he was standing right in front of me. What I could see was that the monument was square, and there was a white stone sculpture on top. I had to peek around both sides of Winston to figure out that the sculpture was a trumpet.

"Who is it?" I asked.

"Another dead guy."

He moved to the side and let me read the name. The first line just said, "*Satchmo*" in script letters. The name right underneath, in block letters, was "Louis Armstrong."

"I've heard of him."

"Greatest horn that ever blew," Winston said.

"He played the trumpet?"

"Now and again, son. Now and again."

"Do you like his music?"

"As long as it's not too darn fast."

"That means you don't like—"

"Shhh!"

"What?"

"I'm communing. It's what us hallucinations do."

"But I thought you were a messenger," I said.

"What? Oh, yeah, right. Messengers do it too."

He craned his neck, stared upward at a cluster of rolling clouds, and took long deep breaths. As he was doing that, I stepped forward for a closer look at the thing. I noticed that the trumpet sculpture was scattered with loose coins, which seemed kind of strange. There were six miniature American flags stuck into the grass at the base of the monument. Behind the row of flags, leaning against the monument, there was a framed black and white photo of a black man in a bow tie sitting next to a black woman. Louis Armstrong had narrow eyes, a big, round face, and a bald head. He also had the widest smile I'd ever seen. I got the feeling that, if we dug him up, that smile would still be plastered across his face, even if the only thing left of his face was a skull.

The thought made me shiver.

After a couple of minutes, Winston took one last deep breath, then stepped back from the grave. "Where to now, Davey?"

"That's it? You're done with the cemetery?"

"We could stroll for a bit. Do a jig or two."

"I'm not going to dance on anybody's grave!"

He let out a sigh. "Have it your way, then."

We walked up and down the rows of monuments and headstones. It felt wrong at first, but soon enough, as weird as it sounds, I started to forget that there were dead people under our feet. It wasn't the worst place to be, reading the engravings and taking photos of the graves. It wasn't boring.

We did that for maybe another half hour. We covered a lot of the cemetery.

That was when Winston pointed toward the mausoleum. "What's in there?"

"It's indoor graves."

"Let's check it out."

"No, I don't want to go in there," I said, then coughed.

"See? You're going to catch your death! C'mon, we can warm up a bit."

"I'm not cold!" I coughed again. "I'm fine out here."

"With this wind blowing right through you?"

"The wind's not blowing through *me*. Oh, yeah, I'm not a hallucination."

"Point taken," he said. "But these specs on my beezer ain't sunglasses."

"Huh?"

"I'm going granite-blind out here, boy."

"There's no such thing as granite-blind!"

"C'mon, Davey, let's go have a look-see."

"I'm not going in there," I said, keeping down another cough.

"Why not?"

"Because it's not right. It's, you know, private."

"But it's all public. It's just outside and inside."

I coughed one more time, a loud deep cough, which gave me time to think. "No," I said. "It's different. Out here, we're…*out here*. We're minding our own business, not bothering anybody. But in there, it's like we don't belong. It's like we're tourists in somebody else's living room."

"But—"

"No!"

"All right," Winston said. "Don't get your knickers in a twist. It just seems a right odd place to draw the line. But, hey, I'm only a figment of your imagination, right? What do I know?"

With that, we turned and headed back toward the gate.

I got a text from Minnie during the walk home. "Are you playing it cool?"

Winston read the message as it came in and jabbed me with his elbow.

I ignored him and wrote back, "Huh?"

"My mom said if you didn't call, that meant you were playing it cool."

"I'm not playing it cool."

"Then why haven't you called?"

"I didn't know I was supposed to call," I wrote. "Why does your mom—"

The phone rang as I was replying. Minnie's name flashed on the screen.

"Hello?"

"My mom says it's a guy thing, playing it cool. But I think it's just rude. It's like a mind-game. You're letting me get worked up, like you want me to feel all emotional, because I'm sitting here, waiting for you to call, and you don't. You know, you're *supposed* to call after a date."

"How was I supposed to know that?"

"Were you just going to wait until tomorrow at school?"

"I really and truly didn't think about it."

"That's even more of an insult!"

"Sorry," I said. I wanted to say more but came up blank.

"Am I your girlfriend?"

"Yes."

"And you're my boyfriend?"

"Yes."

"Do you *mean* that, or are you just *saying* that?"

"No, I mean it. We're boyfriend and girlfriend."

"Then you should call me," she said.

"All right, I will. How often?"

"Whenever you feel like it."

"How often is that?"

"I can't answer that question for you, David."

"But what's a good average?"

The phone cut off. I stared at it in my palm.

"Smooth," Winston said.

I shook my head. "She said I should call her whenever I feel like it. But what does that mean? Once a day? Three times? Five times? Give me a number! Am I supposed to call her as soon as I wake up in the morning? When I get home after school? Before I go to bed? I'll do whatever she wants. It doesn't make a difference to me. *Just tell me!*"

"But what do *you* want, Davey? That's the key."

"I want to call her as often as I'm supposed to."

He shoved me from behind.

"What?" I asked.
"You're a hard case."
"Why?"
"*She just told you the bloody answer,*" Winston said.
"I don't get it."
He smiled. "Call her whenever you feel like calling her."
"We're going around in circles!"
"Call her when you feel like it," he said. "But feel like it often enough to let her know you care."
I looked up at him, and our eyes met. He nodded at me.
I hit the call back button on my phone.
Minnie picked up a second later. "What do you want?"
"I want to talk," I said.
"Why?" she said.
"Just to say hello. To hear your voice."
She laughed. "Now was that so hard?"

Hector and Minnie were waiting for me at the fire hydrant Monday morning. From a block off, I could see they were arguing; her arms were waving, and he kept turning his back to her. Then he caught sight of me; she saw me a second later. They stopped arguing and stiffened up. By the time I got there, they had phony smiles plastered across their faces.
Minnie reached out and grabbed my hand.
"What are you doing?" I asked.
"What do you think I'm doing?"

"Gross!" Hector said, laughing.

She was holding my hand, but I wasn't quite holding hers. It was more like my hand was out there, being held. I could feel the annoyance though her fingertips, so I squeezed her hand, and she squeezed mine back. It was like a conversation without words. After that, no question about it, we were holding hands.

"Are you guys going to walk into the school like that?" Hector asked.

Minnie said, "Why not? I'm not ashamed. Are you ashamed, David?"

"I'm not *ashamed*. But I'm not sure it's a good idea."

She let go of my hand and laughed. "I'm not going to torture you!"

"I'll do it if it means a lot to you. But it's going to attract attention."

"Men!"

That cracked me up, how she sighed as she said it, and Hector was laughing too, and for the first time since I got there, the situation didn't feel awkward. Not that it felt normal either, since I knew Hector's secret, and since I knew that he didn't trust me enough to tell me his secret.

Minnie went her own way once we got inside, and Hector and I went ours, but that not-awkward-but-not-normal feeling hung around. I kept glancing over at him during our classes, and I knew he was glancing over at me since every so often our eyes would meet, and we'd nod at one another, as if we were on the same page, which we *definitely* weren't.

Around three o'clock, as our last class ended, I got a text from Minnie telling me that I shouldn't wait around for her by the hydrant, that she was taking a bus to the mall with a friend. "You don't have to be jealous," she wrote. "It's a girl in my Spanish class. Her name is Angela."

"I'm not jealous," I wrote back.

"I can even send you a photo if you don't believe me."

"I believe you. You don't have to send me a photo."

As I was typing that response, a selfie of the two of them came up. Their heads were tilted together. Minnie had her arm around Angela's shoulders, pulling her in tight—maybe too tight, going by the expression on Angela's face. She had wavy brown hair, a narrow nose, and a nervous smile. She was looking down and off to the left, but Minnie was looking straight at the camera and laughing; she had her mouth wide open and her tongue sticking out, as if to say, *I told you so!*

"Don't worry," Minnie wrote. "We won't talk about you."

Which I knew meant they would.

"Have a good time," I wrote back.

"I think that Satchmo bloke might've cleared some of the muddle," Winston said.

He turned up as soon as I got three blocks away from Talbot, not one step closer.

"What muddle?"

"Me brain!" He twirled his forefinger next to his head. "It's a muddle up there!"

"You figured out what we're supposed to be doing?"

"Some of it," he said. "Nothing like a good commune."

"What did you figure out?"

"Remember how I told you I might be a messenger? Well, I am. No question."

"Good."

"But here's the peculiar bit: so are you."

"*I'm* a messenger?"

"Near as I can figure, yeah," he said.

"Does that mean we're messengers together?"

"Seems likes it. Delivering the message, that's what sets the thing right."

"What thing?"

"Whatever it is we're supposed to set right."

I smacked my forehead.

"Sorry," Winston said.

"What's the message?" I asked.

"Not sure."

"You don't know the message?"

"Not yet, no."

"But how can we be messengers if you don't even know the message?"

"Here's what I know," he said. "The message goes from me to you to the Walrus."

"The *what*?"

"The Walrus…and don't look at me like that."

"Where am I going to find a walrus? Am I supposed to go to the Bronx Zoo?"

"No, I don't think it's an actual walrus. It's more like, you know, a character."

"What kind of character?"

"I wish I knew."

"So you're supposed to tell me a message, and then I'm supposed tell the message to a walrus."

"Not *a* walrus. *The* Walrus."

"Like with a capital W?"

"Yes."

"None of that makes sense!"

"I'm working out the details," Winston said.

"Wait. Who's the message from?"

He shrugged at me. "Not a clue."

"C'mon!" I said. "You don't know what the message is. You don't know who it's from. You *do* know the message is for the Walrus, except you don't know who the Walrus is. Or *what* the Walrus is. I don't want to sound negative, but that's not a lot to go on. Plus, I still don't get why I'm I mixed up in it. I'm like an extra step. Why aren't you hanging around with the Walrus?"

"I wish I could answer that, Davey. That's the part that's still a muddle."

"Wait," I said. "Is it possible that *I'm* the Walrus?"

"It's possible, I guess. But it doesn't sound right."

I shook my head and started to walk faster.

He hustled to catch up. "Let me ask you something then, a real question."

"All right," I said.

"Do you want me to sod off?"

"You mean right now?"

"I mean forever," he said.

"What if I answered yes?"

"Then I think I'd have to sod off."

"Just like that?"

"That's the rule. Don't ask me how I know, but I'm pretty sure you're the boss."

"*I'm* the boss?" I asked.

"I think so."

"Now you tell me!"

"Better late than never," he said. "So what's it going to be?"

I walked another half block as I thought it over. I thought it over good and hard. My feelings were mixed. Not to sound cruel, but the guy was like a piece of gum I couldn't scrape off the bottom of my shoe. On the other hand, he was a guy I could talk to. You need a guy like that. You need a guy who's going to hear you out, who's going to tell you if you're full of crap. I thought Hector was that guy. But if he wasn't going to trust me with his stuff, then I wasn't going to trust him with mine.

I turned to Winston. "You can stay."

"Really?"

"Really."

He threw his arms around my shoulders. "Give us a kiss, then!"

I pushed him off. "C'mon!"

"What made you decide?"

"The main reason," I said, "is I don't want to mess things up for the Walrus. If there is such a person, and if you ever figure out the message. What if I'm the go-between for the two of you? Like that kid in the movie, the one who sees dead people…"

"What movie?"

"You know! 'I see dead people.'"

"You do?"

"Not me! The kid in the movie!"

Winston shrugged. "No idea what you're talking about."

"The movie…where the kid sees dead people and delivers messages from them."

"Ah!"

"Do you know the movie?"

"Sorry, doesn't ring a bell."

"It doesn't matter," I said. "Here's the point. Maybe the Walrus can't see you or hear you, so that's the reason I'm involved. I'm the go-between. Maybe you need me to get the message to him."

"You may be onto something there," Winston said.

"It *is* kind of logical, if you think about it that way."

"Now that's some world class cogitating!"

"But I'm the boss from now on. All right?"

He snapped to attention and saluted with his left hand. "Yes, guvnor."

Even though I was starved by five o'clock, I waited as long as I could for my dad to get home before I ate. By six-thirty, though, I couldn't take it anymore, so I stuck a turkey pot pie in the microwave. I was swallowing the last bite as he came through the front door. He had two Subway sandwiches with him. He looked killed when he poked his head in the kitchen and realized I'd eaten.

He walked over to me and kissed me on top of the head. He smelled of liquor again, though a different kind of liquor than the last time. It was more like a cross between nuts and chocolate, but with that alcohol whiff underneath.

"I should've called and told you," he said. "That's my bad."

"We can put mine in the refrigerator. I'll eat it tomorrow."

"You shouldn't have to eat a cold food all the time."

"The turkey pot pie was hot," I said.

"But before it was hot, it was frozen."

"I don't mind. Really and truly, it tastes just as good."

He plopped down across the table from me. "You want to keep me company?"

"Sure," I said.

"You don't *have* to keep me company. If you've got lots of homework—"

"I don't have lots of homework. I never do. Plus, I want to keep you company."

He unrolled his hero and started to eat.

"Should I get you a soda?" I asked. "We've got Pepsi and Sprite in the fridge."

He looked up and smiled. "Just a glass."

As I got him down a glass from the cupboard, he reached into his pants pocket and pulled out a small squared-off bottle. He poured a gold-colored drink into the glass; the smell of it wafted through the kitchen. It was the nuts and chocolate smell, with the whiff of alcohol.

"What is that?"

"It's called amaretto. Does it smell good to you?"

"It smells like dessert, kind of," I said.

"Yeah, but I'm asking do you *like* the smell?"

I laughed. "Not a lot, no."

He laughed too. "Good."

I sat back down across from him as he continued to eat.

After a couple of minutes of not talking, he said, "It's nice, the two of us, like this."

"Yeah."

"You ever hear of the Marx Brothers?"

"I've heard the name before," I said.

"They were movie stars back in the day. *Way* back in the day. I'm talking about when movies were in black and white. My dad loved those guys. He made me watch their movies with him whenever they were on TV. I must have sat through each movie ten times. I didn't think they were funny at first. But the more I watched with my dad, the funnier they got. We knew them so well, me and my dad, we practically had them by heart. We'd yell the lines out loud to each other. Those were good times, you know? I think maybe it wasn't so much the Marx Brothers; it was because I was watching them with my dad…."

He started to sob but caught himself and took another bite of his hero.

"You want to watch a Marx Brothers movie tonight?" I asked.

"You think they're on Netflix?"

"More likely Amazon," I said.

After he finished the hero, we headed over to the couch in the living room. He fiddled with the remote, which always gave him grief, but after a few minutes he got into the Prime app, and sure enough he found a Marx Brothers movie called *Duck Soup*. He had it up on the screen. But then he turned to me with a sad look. "Do you mind if I shut my eyes for a half hour before we get started? I'm pretty beat."

"I don't mind," I said.

"Yeah, I think a half hour should do me."

"We don't have to watch it tonight."

"No, I want to…"

He muted the TV and rolled back his head to rest it on the back on the couch, and I headed upstairs to my room.

My mom called while I was in the shower on Tuesday morning. I had a hunch it was her, but I didn't want to run back into my room dripping wet, so I let the phone ring. I called her back ten minutes later. Except by then, she was on her way out the door. She said she'd call me back soon.

My dad was still asleep on the couch when I came downstairs. The TV was still on mute. His head was still tilted backward; he hadn't moved the entire night. The only way to tell he was alive was that he was snoring.

I let him sleep.

I got dressed and was about to head out when I got a text from Minnie. It was a heart emoji. Then, a few seconds later, I got another text. "You want to walk to school together?"

"When?" I wrote back.

"Now."

"Where do you want to meet?"

"Your house."

"But I'm on my way out."

"And I'm right outside!"

I swung open the front door. Minnie was on the sidewalk, smiling at me. She gave me a quick, hopeful wave. I closed the door softly behind me, then walked over to her. She leaned in for a kiss, so I kissed her.

"How did you get here?"

"I couldn't fall asleep last night," she said, "so I got up early this morning and walked to school. Except then I didn't feel like waiting around, so I kept walking, and here I am."

"How did you find out my address?"

"I tracked you down on Google."

"Really?"

"Trust me, I *know* how to track people down on Google. I'm a whiz at it. It's the one thing I got from keeping that log for my dad. If you're on the internet, you can't hide from me. You're not freaked out, are you?"

"Why would I be freaked out about that?"

"It's kind of a lurky thing to do."

"What do you mean?"

"*Lurky*. Like I'm lurking behind you, ready to pounce."

"Oh."

"I'm very cat-like, David. You should know that about me. My spirit animal is a leopard. If you're not careful, I might…just…pounce."

She lunged forward and began to tickle me, which made me jump backward.

"Stop!"

"I warned you," she said, laughing.

"C'mon, people can see us."

"We're not doing anything wrong."

"I know. But it's like eight-fifteen."

"What difference does that make?"

"Nobody wants to look out their window in the morning and see a girl tickling a guy."

"I *see*," she said, tapping her chin with her forefinger. "You're saying that if I want to tickle you, I should wait for the afternoon."

"Maybe I don't like being tickled."

"Really?"

"I *don't* like being tickled," I said.

"Then I won't do it anymore."

"Good."

"You're sure you're not freaked out? Because you're hard to read."

"I'm definitely not freaked out," I said.

We started our walk to school.

"Why couldn't you fall asleep?"

"What?"

"You just said you couldn't fall asleep. Why not?"

"I felt horrible ditching you for Angela," she said.

"You didn't ditch me. We didn't have plans."

"Maybe not, but I didn't even get to kiss you after school…unless that's another thing you don't like."

"No, I like kissing."

"Good," she said, "because *that* would be a total deal-breaker."

Might as Well be Dead

Hector's jaw dropped when Minnie and I turned up together, holding hands, at the fire hydrant. He tried to play it off like it was no big deal, but you could tell he was dying to find out what was going on. I was planning to tell him as soon as Minnie headed off to her homeroom, but on second thought, I decided to let him hang.

Fair is fair. He had his secret, and I had mine.

He let it pass until lunch. That was when he broke down and said, "Did Minnie stay over at your house?"

I looked up from my turkey salad. "What do you think?"

"I don't know what to think because you're not talking."

"We can talk about whatever you want to talk about."

Hector narrowed his eyes. "Are you pissed at me?"

"Why would I be pissed at you?"

"The way you said that sounds like you're pissed."

"I'm not pissed at you," I said.

"Then what's going on with you and Minnie?"

"She showed up at my house this morning."

"That's it?"

"She wanted to walk to school together, so we did."

"You need to be careful," he said.

"Careful about what?"

"You like her, right?"

"Yes."

"Do you love her?"

"No!"

"That's what I thought," he said.

"What's your point?"

"If you like her, and she likes you, that's great. Or if you love her, and she loves you. If it's either of those, that's great, and I'm happy for both of you. I mean it. But if you *like* her, and she *loves* you, that's bad. It has to be balanced."

"Or what?"

"Or you're doomed."

"Will you stop saying 'doomed'! I'm not doomed. Nobody is doomed."

As we were going back and forth, neither of us noticed that a girl was standing at the end of the lunch table. How long she'd been standing there, who knew? We would have gone on talking, without realizing she was waiting, if she hadn't said, almost in a whisper, "Excuse me."

Hector and I turned to her at the same time.

Nobody spoke for several seconds.

"You're David Salmon, right?" she asked.

"That's me, yeah."

Her eyes were darting around, like a squirrel's right before it scuttles up the trunk of a tree. Squirrely was how I'd describe her. She was short and kind of hunched in on herself, and her arms were folded over her chest like she was cold. The longer I looked at her face, though, the more familiar she seemed.

"I'm Angela," she said, in a quiet but hopeful way. "Angela Nunzio."

"Pleased to meet you," Hector said.

That was when it hit me. "You're Minnie's friend."

Her eyes finally settled on mine, and she smiled.

"Do you want to eat with us?" I asked.

"No thanks, I already ate."

"Why don't you sit down?" Hector said.

"Could I?"

"It's not *our* table," I said, which sounded more sarcastic than I meant it to sound, so I added, "We're sick of each other anyway."

Hector elbowed me.

She sat down across from Hector, which put her at an angle to me. As soon as she got her legs under the table, she hoisted her backpack onto her lap and began to dig through it. The tip of her tongue was sticking slightly out of the side of her mouth as she did that. Hector and I just watched her.

Finally, she pulled out a sheet of lined paper and handed it to me. It had been folded in half over and over, so unfolding it was like opening a Japanese fan. It read:

Day follows night.
Night follows day.
Who gave you the right
To steal my heart away?

I handed the paper to Hector and looked up at her. I asked, "Did you write this?"

Her eyes widened, and she shook her head. "Me? Oh, no, no!"

I laughed. "You don't have to say it like *that*."

Her face got beet red. "No...I didn't mean...I just meant I didn't write it."

Hector handed the paper back to her; she took it but gave it back to me.

"Who wrote it?" Hector said.

"Minerva. She asked me...I mean...since her lunch isn't till next period..."

Hector turned and shot me a knowing look. Then he summed up the situation just to rub it in. "What you're saying is that Minnie wrote the poem for David, and she asked you to give it to him?"

Angela nodded. It was a fast nod, too fast to look natural, like one of those nodding bobble-head dolls you get at baseball games. But you could see the relief on her face.

Hector whispered to me, "You're doomed."

The rest of the afternoon, I walked around in a kind of brain haze. I was going from class to class, taking notes, but really just writing down random words that came out of the teachers' mouths. Now and then, for no reason, I would unfold the poem and re-read it, and each time I did, I got a sick feeling. It hadn't occurred to me, until the talk with Hector, that Minnie might like me too much, that she might *love* me. That it might be a problem. I mean, I *liked* her. Really and truly, I did. I liked her a lot. I liked being with her. I liked listening to her. I liked kissing her.

But what if she *loved* me?

Even the thought, the sound of the thought, made me queasy.

I waved to Hector after our last class, then rushed out the classroom door, then rushed through the front gate of the school, then rushed past the fire hydrant, and put distance between me and Talbot. Once I got three blocks

Might as Well be Dead

away, I began to glance around for Winston. No sign of him, but I kept walking. Just in case Minnie got it in her head to follow me. After six blocks, I stopped and took a deep breath.

How crazy *was* I?

So what if Minnie was following me? I doubted she was; she would have texted me to wait for her. But even if she came running up the block at that exact moment, what was the worst thing that could happen? I'd ask her why she wrote the poem. She'd tell me that she loved me. It would feel awkward, but so what? It wouldn't be the end of the world. We'd talk it over and get it sorted out. Or not. But even if we didn't get it sorted out, it wouldn't be the end of the world.

No matter what, the world would keep going.

I stood on the corner for five minutes. Not because I thought Minnie was going to turn up, but because I hoped Winston would. Except that was the thing with Winston. He *never* turned up when you hoped he would, when you wanted to get your mind clear, when you needed a distraction. That wasn't his style.

Still, I waited on that corner for five long minutes.

Then I gave up and trudged home.

As soon as I got home, I wolfed down the leftover Subway hero. I wasn't even very hungry, but I wolfed it down regardless. I wanted to be done with dinner before my dad came through the door, just in case he had another

Marx Brothers night planned. I had too much on my mind.

I headed upstairs, shut the door to my room, sat on the edge of my bed, and waited. *Something* was going to happen; I could feel it. Either Winston was going to show up, since I hadn't seen him the entire day, or my mom was going to call back, since we hadn't gotten to talk that morning, or Minnie was going to text, or call, or maybe even ring the doorbell. If she rang the doorbell, that would be a bad sign.

I put down the phone on the mattress next to me.

Not a minute passed before the phone began to vibrate; the vibration came through the mattress, and I felt it up and down my body. I flipped the phone over to see the number.

The call was from Minnie.

"Hello?" I said.

"You sound upset."

"I'm not upset."

"Please don't lie to me, David."

"I'm not lying."

"Why did you run off after school?"

"I was in a hurry to get home."

"Why?"

"Because I wanted to eat dinner before my dad got home. I didn't want to watch the Marx Brothers."

"I don't know what that means," she said.

"It means I was in a rush."

"Are you upset because of my poem?"

"No!"

"Well…"

"Well what?"
"What's your reaction to it?"
"It was a good poem," I said.
"That's it? That's your reaction?"
"What do you want me to say?"
There was a long pause.
Then, at last, she said, "*Guys*!"
"Guys, what?"
"Guys…they keep their feelings bottled up."
"I don't think—"
"C'mon, David, you're like the poster boy."
"Just because—"
"You don't have to worry," she said. "I see you in there. Your secret is safe."
"What secret?"
"That you have feelings. You don't have to talk about them. We can drop it."

I was about to answer but changed my mind; dropping it felt like a good idea.

There was another long pause.

Then Minnie said, "So when will it be all right for my mom to call your dad?"

"I don't know if that's such a good idea."

"Why not? You said he was having a hard time. My mom might cheer him up."

"He needs time, I think."

"David, my mom is *very* sensitive. She's not going to be pushy or anything."

"Then what's the rush?"

"There's no rush. But I think she's really into him, and they might hit it off."

"I just don't…my dad's not thinking about that kind of stuff. It's too soon."

"But wouldn't it be neat if they were dating *and* we were dating?" she said.

"Why would that be neat?"

"Then maybe they'd get married…."

"That's gross!" I said.

"Why are you saying that?"

"If they got married, we'd be step-brother and step-sister."

That made her laugh. "All right, I get your point. But I still think it might be good for both of them."

My dad rolled in around eight o'clock and called upstairs, "You ate already, right?" I called down that I had, and that covered our conversation for the night. I watched TV for a couple of hours, and during commercials knocked off about a half hour of homework, then washed up and slid into bed. Before I shut my eyes, though, my mom called. She asked if I had time to chat, and I fought back a yawn and told her I did.

"What do you want to chat about?" I asked.

"Well, how are things going with Minnie?"

"They're fine, I guess."

"That doesn't sound very convincing."

"She wrote me a poem…."

"Oh, David! You've got her hooked!"

"Except what am I supposed to do?"

"David…"

"Please don't tell me to follow my heart."

"Following your heart is well and good," she said. "But you also need to think about what you're doing. Minnie is dear to you, isn't she? I don't need to remind you that her feelings are precious things. You need to be careful with them."

"Don't I have to be honest with her?"

"Well, *of course* you do! But that doesn't get you out of your responsibility to be kind. You can be both, you know. Honest *and* kind. But that means you have to be sensitive. You have to think about what you say and do."

"Minnie's mom…I think she's got a crush on Dad."

"What?" She began to laugh. "Is *that* the problem?"

"But Dad is—"

"He's a grown man, David."

"But you don't know what it's like for him."

"David, he's stronger than you think he is."

"No, he isn't," I said. "You don't even talk to him."

"I have my ways of checking up without talking to him. You're one of them."

"You think he's ready to go out on a date?"

"Probably not," she said. "But that's his decision to make, not yours or mine."

"Is that what you want?"

"What I want is for him to be happy. The only way he's going to be happy is if he moves on with his life. I'm moving on, and you're moving on. Don't you think he deserves that chance too?"

Might as Well be Dead

Hector called *way* too early on Wednesday morning, an hour before I had to wake up, to tell me he had a stomach flu and was going to miss school. But of course, he couldn't leave it at that. He had to paint a word picture. You know…the kind of word picture you're *dying* to hear at six-thirty in the morning.

By the time he finished, *I* was feeling sick.

"You'll text me your notes, right?"

"Sure," I said, praying for no more details.

"David, I *need* you to take good notes."

"I'll take notes."

"*Good* notes, especially in history."

"I'll take good notes in history," I said.

I was wide awake when we hung up, and I was annoyed. Not so much because he'd called early, or because he'd grossed me out, but because I knew what he was doing: he was forcing me to pay attention in our classes. He was using his stomach flu to get me to listen to our teachers.

Since I was up early anyway, I took a long, hot bath instead of a shower. I kept the light off in the bathroom; it was gray and shadowy when I slid into the tub, and over the next half hour, I watched the sunrise seep in the window and cut into the steamy air. Birds were chirping in the trees right outside, but they never got too loud. Just enough to keep me from thinking too much.

My dad was asleep on the couch when I came downstairs. He'd taken off his shoes and socks, but he still had on his pressed pants and button-down shirt from the day before. He also had on his red tie; he hadn't even loosened the knot. He'd flung his suit jacket in the direction of the rocking chair but missed. It was billowed out on the floor between two open boxes of my mom's stuff. I walked over to the couch and stared at him. He looked real peaceful at first, but then, without warning, his shoulders hunched up, and he grabbed at the sides of his head. It was like a seizure, that's how sudden and violent it was. Except a second later, it was over. His shoulders relaxed, and his arms slipped down to his sides.

It occurred to me right then that *he* was the one who needed therapy, not me. I knew there was no chance he would go on his own. But, maybe, if I told him *I* needed it, I could get him to come along.

It was a thought.

He continued to sleep as I toasted a couple of frozen waffles and downed a glass of orange juice. Then I headed back upstairs and got dressed. He was starting to move around as I pulled on my coat. I said goodbye in a soft voice and slid the door shut as quietly as I could.

Winston was nowhere to be found as I walked to Talbot. I hadn't seen him since Monday afternoon, which meant he'd gone missing for a day and a half. Who knew what the guy was up to? (Yeah, I know.) As much as I hated to admit it, the walk to school felt longer without him. I was still looking for him when I saw Minnie standing at the fire hydrant. I walked up to her and leaned in for a kiss, but she pulled her head back. That caught me off guard. "What are you mad about?"

"I'm not mad at you, David. I'm just giving you more space."

"Space for what?"

"Space for whatever," she said. "I think you feel crowded."

"I didn't say I felt crowded."

"You didn't say it with *words*."

"If I felt crowded, I'd say it with words."

"If you *knew* you felt crowded," she said.

"How could I feel crowded and not know it?"

"You tell me...."

I took a long, deep breath. "Hector's out sick."

"I figured that out."

"You're sure you're not mad?" I asked.

"No, I'm not mad."

We walked together the last block to the school gate. I wondered the entire time if I was supposed to kiss her when we headed to our homerooms, or maybe squeeze her hand, or maybe just nod. What did "more space" mean? I got my answer as we passed through the double doors. She reached out with her thumb and forefinger, grabbed one of the belt loops on my pants, and gave it a quick tug. That was it; she just tugged on one of my belt loops. From that, I got the sense that even if she was annoyed, she wasn't *mad*.

I yawned through homeroom, but as soon as I got to first period English, I took good notes for Hector's sake. Whatever Mrs. Voros said about Emily Dickinson, if it sounded even slightly important, I wrote it down. About a half hour into the class, Mrs. Voros glanced over at me, and our eyes met, and she nodded, as if she were saying, *nice to see you're back, David.* It burned me, how she nodded, and I almost put down my pen, but how could I do that after I'd promised Hector? So I kept going. It was like that all morning, in every class. I was a note-taking fool, and the more notes I took, the more teachers nodded and smiled at me, and the more annoyed I got. I was knocking myself out for the guy, and he didn't even trust me with his secret.

By lunch period, I was steamed. I stood in line for my veggie sandwich, then took the tray over to our usual table…except it was just me. Just me and my thoughts. I took a couple of bites, then put the sandwich down and scanned the cafeteria. I caught sight of Angela, sitting by herself at a table near the emergency exit. I picked up my lunch tray and headed over to her.

"You mind if I eat with you?" I asked.

She brushed aside a swirl of brown hair hanging on her forehead. "Where's Hector?"

"Out sick."

"I don't mind," she said.

I set my tray on the table and sat down across from her. "Why are you eating alone?"

"I like to think, I guess."

"You always eat alone?"

"Most of the time," Angela said. "But I've got friends, if that's what you're asking."

"I wasn't asking that."

She pointed past my left shoulder. "Those three girls over there, at the third table, I eat with them sometimes."

I didn't turn around. "You don't have to prove it. I trust you."

"I'm just saying you don't have to feel sorry for me," she said.

"Look, Hector is out sick, and I don't feel like eating alone."

"What's he out sick with?"

"You don't want to know."

"Is it something serious?"

"No, it's something gross," I said.

"Oh. Sorry."

"You're in Minnie's…math class?"

"No, her Spanish class," she said.

"Do you sit next to her?"

"Right behind her. I said hello."

"Why did you do that?"

"She's upbeat. I like that."

"I like that too," I said.

"I'm not upbeat. It's not me."

"Me either."

"Yeah, I noticed," she said.

That felt like an insult, even though I knew she didn't mean it that way.

Neither of us spoke for the next few seconds. It got to be painful, so I blurted out, "Do you have a boyfriend?"

"No!"

"Why are you saying it like that?"

"It's fine for you and Minerva," she said. "It's just not for me."

"Why not?"

"Because I'm not in a hurry."

"I wasn't in a hurry," I said.

"I *said* it was fine for you and Minerva. I'm not judging you. It's just not something I think a lot about."

"I never thought about it either," I said, "until it happened."

"But you were ready, right?"

"Truthfully, I never thought about it one way or the other."

"Does it make you happy?"

"I don't know. I guess. Sometimes, when I think about it."

"You're happy when you think about it?"

"Yeah."

"What about when you're with Minerva?"

"It's all right," I said. "It's…I guess it's just pressure."

It was one of those conversations where you get out ahead of what you're saying, so you're talking and listening at the same time, deciding whether what you're saying makes sense. *I had a girlfriend.* What did that even mean? Minnie Drugas was my girlfriend, and I was her boyfriend. We were boyfriend and girlfriend. Which meant, what? That I had to talk on the phone more than before and get a few more text messages? That I got to hold her hand and kiss her? That I ate her pralines but worried that her mom had a crush on my dad? If you did the math, and you put the good things on one side and the bad things on the other, what did the equation look like?

I was still doing that math during math class in the afternoon, which made it hard to take good notes for

Hector. I focused as much as I could on the teacher and blackboard, and on my pen and notebook, but I kept hearing Angela's voice: "Does it make you happy?" The words cut through me.

That *had* to be the bottom line, didn't it?

After final period, I headed out and waited for Minnie at the fire hydrant. It took her longer than usual to get there, but I figured I should wait after how weird our conversation was that morning.

She came out five minutes later. She was with a cluster of girls I didn't know; they were laughing and talking a mile a minute. Whatever trouble she'd had making friends, she had past it. When she noticed me waiting at the hydrant, she waved, and a few seconds later, she started to shake loose from the cluster of girls. But it took a while. She had to hug each one of them, then take a couple of steps toward me, then rush back and whisper something to the nearest one. She did that three times before she broke free.

I had my arms crossed over my chest as she got close. I didn't mean anything by it, though it might have come off like I was tired of waiting for her. She was walking slowly, but then she rushed forward, threw her arms around my neck, and kissed me on the lips. She caught me so off guard that the two of us almost tumbled backward. It was a different kind of kiss, the kind of kiss you see in movies, where a guy and his girlfriend get reunited after being apart for like ten years…or where they realize they're *going* to be apart for ten years. But the entire time we were kissing, she had my arms pinned against my chest, so I couldn't even hug her back.

When it was over, when she pulled back, I heard a loud, "*Whoooo!*"

It came from the cluster of girls.

They were laughing and pointing and giving her thumbs-up signs.

"What did you do that for?" I asked.

"Because we're a couple, aren't we?"

"Yeah, but—"

She got a sad look on her face. "What's wrong? Didn't you like it?"

"It's not that," I said. "But why did you do it in front of everybody?"

"Don't you like PDAs?"

"What?"

"Public displays of affection," she said. "You're being so *uptight*, David!"

"I'm not uptight."

She grabbed my face between her hands and laughed. "Be free!"

Winston came up behind me six blocks into the walk home. It was the first time he'd shown his face since Monday. I caught sight of his shadow on the sidewalk as he got close; the shape of it caused me to smile. Shoulders hunched forward. Long strides. Hands in his pockets.

I stopped and waited. "Where have you been?"

"Running errands, mostly."

"Oh, right," I said. "What kind of errands?"

"Just errands. You know how it is."

"For example?"

"Laundry, for example. That sort of thing."

"*You* do laundry?"

"I'm not saying I do it myself," he said. "I'm not saying I take my clothes down to the river and beat them against rocks. I drop them off at the shop, and I pick them up the next day."

"What shop is that?"

"The laundry shop."

"The laundry *shop*?"

"That's right," he said.

"What's its name?"

He grinned. "Liberty."

"Liberty, what?"

"Liberty Wash," he said. "Give me your tired, your poor, your faded undies yearning to be bleached."

"So you're not going to tell me where you were?"

"I could tell you, but then I'd have to shoot you."

"Fine!"

"What's going on with your bird?" he asked.

"Bird meaning girlfriend."

He nodded. "Changing your world, is she?"

"It's not that. She's just, you know, upbeat."

"Upbeat, you say! Well, then! Say no more!"

"It's too much sometimes," I said.

"I once had a mate like that. Not a bad sort, but bloody irksome."

"It gets on your nerves."

"Especially since you're…you know."

I eyed him up and down. "I'm what?"

"Not so upbeat."

"But I'm not *down*beat," I said. "I'm just normal. Regular beat."

"If you say so."

"I *am*."

"Except with a screw loose, right?"

"Look, it's one thing if I say it—"

"The rules are the rules," he said.

"Did you figure out anything else about the Walrus?"

"Nothing new," he said. "But the whole thing will come clear soon enough. I can feel it whirling around, waiting for me to make sense of it."

As soon as I got home, I scanned the notes I'd taken and texted them to Hector. All I wrote was, "Here you go." I put that in first message and left it at that. A minute after the last page, I got back a text from Hector that read, "Thanks!" That's it. One word. Not, "Nice job on the notes!" or "You went to a lot of trouble!" Just "Thanks!"

I guess I should've been grateful for the exclamation point.

Hector texted again at seven-forty-five on Thursday morning to say he was going to miss another day of school. He didn't ask me to take more notes, but I knew that was what he wanted. I thought about what I should write back, and I came up with an exclamation point. So

I texted him an exclamation point. Nothing else. No words. Just an exclamation point.

I got back a question mark.

I texted him back *three* exclamation points.

I got back three question marks…which cracked me up.

That ended our chat.

While I was in the shower, Minnie texted. She asked if I wanted her to wait for me at the fire hydrant. Except I didn't get the message; I didn't hear the phone ping because of the water in my ears. I got dressed, headed downstairs, downed a bowl of cereal, then headed back upstairs. That was when I noticed her text. I wrote back, "Yes." But I got no answer. I slid on my backpack and went back downstairs.

By then, my dad had wandered out of his bedroom and was puttering around the kitchen in his bathrobe.

"You want eggs?" he called to me.

I pulled on my coat. "Already ate."

"How'd you get so independent?"

"Practice, I guess."

I stepped outside and pulled the door shut behind me.

Winston didn't show up on the walk to school, and Minnie wasn't standing at the fire hydrant. I waited for her for five minutes until the warning bell rang; then I hustled through the front gate, through the double doors, past the security guard, up one flight of stairs, and down the long hallway to homeroom.

I got a good long stare from Mrs. Pang, who'd already started to take attendance.

On my way to first period English, I texted Minnie that I'd waited for her at the fire hydrant, but I got no answer. I headed to class and set my phone on vibrate. I checked a few times while Mrs. Voros was talking, but Minnie hadn't written back. That was when it hit me that she was mad.

But what could I do?

I put her out of my mind the rest of the morning. What I concentrated on was taking more notes for Hector; I even started to like it, kind of. It felt like the more notes I took, the more I was winning an argument. Except I was arguing with myself, not with Hector. Even so, I filled up page after page of full sentences in neat, legible print. Going by the last two days, you'd think I was writing an encyclopedia.

When I got to the cafeteria for lunch, I glanced over at Angela's table, but she wasn't there, so I figured I'd have to eat alone. But then, after I'd stood in line for my pizza square and salad, I found *her* sitting at *my* table. I slid down across from her. She looked up at me and smiled weakly.

"Hector's out sick again," I said.

"I know. Minerva told me."

"Did she tell you to eat with me?"

"She doesn't tell me who to eat with."

"Then why—"

"You said you didn't like to eat alone."

"That's right," I said. "I don't."

"I cut to the chase."

"What chase?"

She sighed. "You were going to come over to my table, right?"

"I was thinking about it."

"Well, I came over to yours instead. It's less awkward that way."

"Except now it's *really* awkward."

"I was just thinking that," she said, and her smile got bigger.

"You're saying you came over because you felt sorry for me?"

"That's not what I'm saying. I'm saying I like talking to you."

"Why?"

She leaned back and folded her hands on the table. "Do you want me to leave?"

"No," I answered. "I *don't* like to eat alone. But I thought *you* liked to eat alone."

"Why do you think that?"

"Because you *told* me you liked to eat alone."

"Yeah," she said, "but I was making a point."

"What point?"

"I was saying you don't have to feel sorry for me."

"I don't have to feel sorry for you," I said, "and you don't have to feel sorry for me."

"Right!"

"I'm glad we've cleared that up."

That made her laugh. It was a soft laugh, almost like a whisper of a laugh. She shook her head, and that swirl of brown hair fell onto her forehead. She pushed it back a couple of times, but it kept falling.

"Why don't you leave it alone?"

"Leave what alone?" she said.
"Your hair. It looks good loose."
She left it alone and gave me a hard look. "You think so?"
"I wouldn't say so if I didn't think so."
"Thank you for saying so," she said.
I took a bite of my pizza, and she took a bite of her grilled chicken sandwich.
She swallowed her bite first. "I think Minerva has beautiful hair. I wish my hair was as straight as hers; I'd grow it down to my hips maybe. I'm not so crazy about the blue streak though. Why would she do that?"
"She said she needed a change."
"It's not a catastrophe, but I'm still not crazy about it."
"Does she ever talk to you about pralines?" I asked.
"What?" She cracked up. "No!"
"Then what do you talk about?"
"That's between the two of us."
"Do you know her new friends?"
"What new friends?"
"I guess that answers that," I said.
She eyed me suspiciously. "Are you pumping me for information?"
"No!"
"Then why are you asking me all these questions about Minerva?"
"I'm just making conversation."

After school, instead of going straight to the fire hydrant, I waited for Minnie outside the front gate. She came out a couple of minutes later with the same group of girlfriends as the day before. There were six of them, counting Minnie; they were like one shape-shifting thing, like a swarm, like a protoplasm oozing along the sidewalk. None of them noticed me until the group had swallowed me, until Minnie and I were face to face in the midst of them.

"You're here!" she said, looking up.

"So are you."

The rest of the girls started to chant, "Kiss! Kiss! Kiss!"

She cut them off. "David's not into PDAs!"

It made me cringe; I knew the looks that would follow.

Those were the looks I got

Minnie grabbed me by the hand, and the two of us pulled free of the group. Then we walked together in the direction of the fire hydrant. We were still holding hands but not speaking.

Then, as we got to the hydrant, I said, "Why do your friends want us to kiss?"

"Because it's romantic."

"Then let them get their own boyfriends."

"They *have* their own boyfriends," she said. "But it's still a romantic thing."

"Why?"

"Because they think it's our happily-ever-after. Like at the end of a movie."

"Yeah, I remember. But why do we need a happily-ever-after?"

"Because of you, David…because of, you know, *the thing that happened*."

"What happened?"

"You know," she said. "With your mom."

"Oh, come on!"

"They're rooting for you. Is that really so bad? They're rooting for *us*."

"Let them root for the Mets instead," I said.

"I don't understand why you're being like this."

"I'm not being like *this*. I'm being like me."

"I know you like to keep things private, but—"

"This is me."

"Yes, but when you keep things locked up—"

"Except there's no 'but.' They're *my* things."

She stared at me and let out a deep breath.

"What are you trying to say?" she asked.

"I'm not trying to say anything."

"Don't you want a happily-ever-after?"

"Not if it means kissing in front of your friends," I said. "That's not who I am."

"Then who are you?"

"I'm a guy who's hanging on. All right?"

"I know," she said. "I'm a girl who's hanging on. Can't we hang on together?"

"Maybe you need to let go."

She put her hands over her mouth, and her eyes welled up. I felt bad, but I stood there and watched her. The first tears rolled out of her eyes a second later. She waited for the tears to come, and for me to get a good, long look at them. Then she turned and ran back to her friends.

I turned and started to walk home.

Might as Well be Dead

"You really made a shambles of that," Winston said.

He was walking backward on the sidewalk in front of me, peeking over his shoulder every few seconds to make sure he wasn't going to stumble over the curb. It was weird to think of him tripping and falling, like that was possible, but he seemed worried about it. I would have paid to see it happen.

"I don't care."

"She'll scrub her hands of you for sure."

"If she does, she does. It's her decision."

"Well, well, look who's a leather-hearted git!"

"I never asked for a girlfriend," I said.

He nodded. "Problem solved then, eh?"

"What was I supposed to do?"

"There's no *supposed to*," he said.

"Then why are you getting on my case?"

"There's nothing you can do but learn how to be you."

"You know who you sound like? The Cat in the Hat."

"You mean because it rhymes?"

"No, because it's corny," I said.

"That Cat in the Hat sounds like my kind of cat."

"Now you're doing it on purpose."

He spun around to walk forward. "Would I, could I, in reverse?"

I smiled. "You'll always do whatever's worse."

"Now you're getting the hang of it, Davey Boy!"

Neither of us spoke for the next block as I put together a thought.

Then, at last, I said, "Maybe she's too upbeat."

"Maybe so."

"I mean, if we don't fit, then we don't fit. So why draw it out?"

"Sounds like you're trying to convince yourself of something."

"You think I should call her, or wait and see what happens?"

"I've got you pegged as more the wait-and-see sort," he said.

"I don't want to hurt her feelings."

"I'm a-feared that ship has sailed."

Hector called as I shut the front door behind me. It was like he had a sensor, like he knew I was planning to run upstairs, peel off my clothes, and flop down on my bed…and not answer the phone. He got me before I could let go, before I could slide off my backpack, so I answered the phone because it rang, without thinking about it.

"Yes," I said, "I took lots of notes."

"Hello to you too."

"How do you feel?"

"Still queasy, but not like before."

"You going to school tomorrow?"

"I think so, yeah" he said. "But what happened with Minnie?"

"Nothing happened with Minnie."

"She was crying when she got home. I saw her out the window."

"You spend a lot of time looking out your window?"

"Yes, I do," he said. "Do you have a problem with that?"

"I don't have a problem with anything you do," I said.

"Good."

"I'll text you the notes tonight."

"Good."

I ran upstairs, peeled off my clothes, and flopped down on my bed. Except now, once I landed on the bed, I had to fight off the thought of Minnie crying as she walked home. I couldn't do it. I could picture her crying the entire way, every step of every block, running the last few steps to her house, running past her mom, running into her room, flopping down onto her bed, and sobbing into her pillow. I could *hear* her sobs. Meanwhile, I was lying on my back, with my arms straight down my sides, not moving an inch, like a corpse in a coffin. How did I get to be the bad guy?

I shouldn't have eaten her pralines.

I wasn't feeling good about Friday even before I woke up. The last hour I was asleep, I kept dreaming about taking more notes for Hector, and the teacher in every class was doing a lesson on how I'd hurt Minnie's feelings. The first thing I did when I opened my eyes was call my mom. It was five minutes before seven, which I knew was too early to call, but I couldn't stop myself. I had to hear her voice.

"What's the matter, sweetie?" she said, sounding groggy.

"Did I wake you up?"

"Yes, but it's all right. I had to wake up in ten minutes."

"I don't think I have a girlfriend anymore."

"I'm so sorry...."

"The thing is, I don't think I was very nice to her," I said.

She hesitated, then said, "David, you're a sensitive, intelligent young man. You know right from wrong. If you don't think you were very nice, then you probably *weren't* very nice. Do you want to tell me what happened?"

"No."

"Do you want me to forgive you?"

"No."

"That's good because you know it's not my forgiveness that matters."

"I know."

"You need Minnie's forgiveness, and then maybe you need your own."

"I know. It's just that—"

"David, are you talking to me, or are you talking to yourself? You know I'm on your side, whatever you do. That's not going to change. But if you need to make something right, make it right."

We said our goodbyes, and I hung up the phone.

I felt pretty low as I got out of bed.

Hector was waiting for me at the fire hydrant, but Minnie wasn't with him. As I got there, he stepped forward and put out his right hand. I stared down at his hand, unsure what he was doing.

"Seriously, David?" he asked. "You're going to leave me hanging?"

We shook hands; it felt real self-conscious, at least on my end.

"What's that for?"

"I owe you."

"For what?"

"You took very good notes. I'm sure it must have been a pain."

"It wasn't a big deal," I said.

"What did you say to Minnie?"

"What did she tell you I said?"

"She wouldn't talk about it. That's why I'm asking you."

"We got into a fight because I didn't want to kiss her."

"If you don't want to kiss her—"

"*In public*," I said. "I don't want to kiss her *in public*."

He smiled. "Well, that's different."

"It's just that I don't want people looking at us…at me."

"Yeah, you're like that." He smiled again, even wider.

"It's not funny," I said. "I think I hurt her feelings."

"You don't have to *think* about it. You definitely did."

"How do I fix things?"

"I don't think you can fix things," he said. "If she wants you to feel a certain way, and you don't feel that way, that's not fixable. But you need to talk to her about it. You shouldn't pretend nothing happened. That's disrespectful."

"What should I say to her?"

"You could start by telling her what you told me, how you don't like people looking at you."

"I already told her that!"

"In those exact words?"

"No," I said.

"Try those exact words."

As soon as I sat down in homeroom, before Mrs. Pang began her announcements, I texted Minnie. I asked her if we could talk after school. Then I slid my phone into my pants pocket and waited for it to buzz with her answer.

No answer came during homeroom, so I stashed the phone and headed with Hector to first period American History. I must have checked for Minnie's answer ten times during class. Nothing showed up.

I kept checking the entire morning, but Minnie was ghosting me. She had to be doing it on purpose; no way would she go that long without looking at her phone. By the time lunch period rolled around, I'd gotten used to the idea. She was ghosting me, and Winston was ghosting me. But in different ways.

What could I do? I was ghost-able.

"Still nothing?" Hector asked, as we headed for the cafeteria.

"Still nothing."

"Give it time."

"But if *she's* ghosting *me*, isn't she being disrespectful too?"

"It's only been a day since you talked to her. Give it time."

We sat down at our usual table for lunch and were chatting away. Really, it was the first time in a long time I wasn't annoyed at Hector…because, well, because he was still Hector, even if he didn't trust me with his secret. When he told me to *give it time*, that had two meanings for me.

Several minutes later, Angela showed up. She slid her tray down across from me and smiled. But the look on her face was different. It was stiff. I thought she might feel awkward since it wasn't just the two of us, so I turned to Hector and said, in a casual way, "Angela eats with us now."

She turned to Hector, "If that's all right."

Hector leaned toward her. "Absolutely."

"I have something to tell you," she said.

"Both of us?" I asked.

She turned back to me. "No, just you."

"What is it?"

"It's a message. It's from Minerva." She glanced at Hector, then back at me. "Should I say it out loud or whisper it?"

"You can say it out loud," I said.

"She wants me to break up with you."

I stared at her as the words sank in.

"That came out wrong," she said. "Minerva wants me to tell you she wants to break up with you."

"Why wouldn't she tell me that herself?"

"She wants to meet you after school to talk."

"Then why are you telling me now?" I asked.

"Because you texted her. She didn't want you to feel confused."

"Why didn't she text me back and say she wanted to break up?"

"Because she didn't want to break up by text."

"So instead, she sent *you* to break up with me?"

"*I don't know*," Angela said. "I guess maybe she thought it would feel more personal if I told you. You know, because I'm a *person*. But you need to ask her. I'm only delivering the message."

"She must have said something else. Did she tell you why she wants to break up?"

Hector elbowed me. Not too hard, but he got my attention. When I looked over at him, he was shaking his head.

"Do you want me to leave?" Angela said.

"What do you mean?"

"Do you want me to eat at another table?"

"No!"

"You're sure?"

"Yes, I'm sure," I said.

"You're not mad at me for telling you?"

"Why would I be mad at you?"

"Didn't you ever hear the saying, 'shoot the messenger'?"

"Except you're not *just* the messenger. You're also my friend."

That caught Angela off guard. You could tell from how she reacted. She looked straight at me for a second, then glanced to the side and started to blush.

"Trust me," I said, "I know what it's like to be the messenger. You don't get to choose the message."

"Thank you," she mumbled.

Hector reached across the table and patted the top of her hand. He gave her a sincere look. "You can eat with us whenever you want, but just so you know, we're pretty boring."

Angela laughed at that.

The shock that Minnie had sent Angela to break up with me left me numb. It wasn't a bad feeling; it had a nice finality to it, and it meant that I didn't have to think any more about whether I wanted a girlfriend. But as the afternoon wore on, that numb feeling wore off, and what took its place was dread. The fact that Minnie wanted to *talk* about our breakup, *that* I was dreading.

But I knew there was no weaseling out of it, so I waited for her at the fire hydrant after school.

She came outside alone, which was a relief. I didn't want her new cluster of friends hanging around the front gates, watching our conversation from a distance. She kept her eyes down as she walked toward me, like she was curious where her every step landed on the sidewalk. She didn't look up until she got to the fire hydrant. She had a sad smile on her face when she did.

"I'm so sorry, David. I shouldn't have asked Angela to do that."

"You could've waited and told me yourself."

"I realize that. Do you think it was a totally awful thing to do?"

"I don't think it was awful. It was just weird."

"I guess I just…I just wanted you to know as soon as possible."

"That makes sense."

"You don't think I'm a terrible person?"

"No!"

"It's nothing against you," she said. "You're a great guy. It's just that I feel like we're in different places. Like I'm ready for something, and you're not. Not that you should be. It's just…"

"Just what?"

"It's just, you know, timing. But there's no right time and wrong time. It's a personal thing. I don't know if I'm explaining it the right way."

"You don't have to explain it. It's not a big deal."

"You see? That's exactly what I'm talking about."

"What do you mean?" I asked.

"I'm breaking up with you, but I'm more upset than you are."

"Maybe I just don't show it."

"C'mon, David! Is that true?"

"No."

"Let's at least be honest about what's going on," she said. "I'm pouring my heart out, and you're like *whatever*. I mean, is this upsetting you at all? Do you understand what breaking up means?"

"It means we're not boyfriend and girlfriend anymore."

"But *emotionally*. Do you even understand what's happening?"

"Well, yeah."

"Are you going to miss me?"

"It's not like we'll never see each other. We still go to the same school. I'll still see you all the time."

She grabbed my face with both her hands and brought her face right up to mine. The tips of our noses were about a half inch apart. "Are you going to miss me?"

"I just told you—"

She kissed me hard on the lips, then let go.

"Are you going to *miss me*?"

"Oh, *that*," I said. "Yeah, I'll miss you for sure."

"Oh God! What am I going to do with you? You're the sweetest guy I've ever known, and you're the most frustrating guy I've ever known."

"I'm not trying to be."

"I know you're not," she said. "That's the frustrating part."

She let go of my face and stepped back. Then she smiled.

"So are we going to be friends?" I asked.

She let out a deep breath. "I'd like that."

Winston was sitting on the desk chair in my room when I got home. But *sitting on* it wasn't what he was doing. It was more like he was surrounding it, straddling it backward with his legs folded around the backrest and his arms crossed over the top and his chin nested in his arms.

I flung my backpack onto my bed and sat down on the edge of the mattress.

Winston twisted his head sideways, like he was expecting me to talk first.

"What?" I asked.

"Now what?"

"Now what, what?"

"Now that you're a bachelor again," he said, "what's your next move?"

"I don't have a next move. Why do I need a next move?"

"That Angela bird seems keen on you."

"Why do you say that?"

"I've just got a feeling," he said.

"Even if she is—"

"Plus, she's got a good name."

It took me a second to realize what he meant. "You're *not* an angel."

"Yeah, yeah, yeah."

"But you're not."

"I don't have a union card, no."

"Besides," I said, "she already told me she doesn't want a boyfriend."

"Do you want a girlfriend?"

"I don't know. Probably not."

"Sounds to me like the two of you belong together," he said.

"Because we both don't want the same thing?"

"No question about it."

My dad rolled in around nine o'clock. I was still upstairs when I heard him push open the front door. He walked straight across the living room and then up the stairs. His footsteps sounded quick and decisive at first, but as he got closer to the top, they slowed down; whatever was on his mind, it was like you could hear him starting to rethink it. It was a sad sound.

His knock against my bedroom door was even sadder.
"Yeah," I said.
He pushed open the door. "So about tomorrow…"
"What about tomorrow?"
"Look, I don't think I can make it," he said.
"Make what?"
"Temple."
"Temple?"
"We were supposed to go to temple together."
"Oh, yeah," I said.
"You forgot about it?"
I smiled at him. "Kind of."
"It's a serious thing."
"I know. I'm sorry. But we can go next week."
"No way," he said. "You can go on your own."
"But I thought the whole point was for us—"
"Look," he said, "I'm just not feeling it now."
"All right."
"But I think you should go. For both of us."
"But that doesn't make any sense," I said.
"David, you and I need a *foundation*…."
"Yeah, both of us. Why should I go alone?"

"Look," he said, "what's the big deal? You wake up. You put on your suit. You get in an Uber. You slap on a yarmulke and sit in temple for a couple of hours. You get back in an Uber. You still got most of the day ahead of you."

"Then why can't we go together?"

"I just told you. I'm not *feeling* it."

"What if I'm not feeling it either?"

He took a deep breath and rubbed his right palm into his forehead. "Look, I'm *asking* you to do this for us. For both of us. I'm not *telling* you that you have to do it. But it would mean a lot to me if you did it. You can make up your own mind."

He shuffled out of my room and slid the door closed slowly behind him.

"He did you up right and proper," Winston said, back in the desk chair.

"It's stupid."

"But you're going, right?"

"What choice do I have?"

"Ah, you're a good lad."

"You'll come with me, won't you?"

"Wouldn't miss it," he said.

I woke up, if you want to call it that, before sunrise on Saturday morning. I'm not sure I ever fell asleep. Either I was half-asleep, dreaming about the moment I had to get out of bed and put on my suit, or I was half-awake, dreading the moment I had to get out of bed and put on my suit. All I knew for sure was that I had to put on my suit. How had I wound up in this mess? The whole point of going to temple was my dad wanted to go. That was the reason I didn't mind. It was the only reason I said yes. I thought maybe it would do him good, light a fire under him. I mean, *he* was the one whose life had ground to a halt. Why was I the one who had to put on that stupid suit?

Sunlight began to come into the room, and I closed my eyes. It didn't help. Even with my eyes shut tight, the sun got in. Once it got in the room, it got inside my eyelids; I could see orange where a minute before I'd seen only black.

I opened my eyes again, threw off the covers, and got out of bed.

The shower I took was the longest I'd ever taken. You know how shampoo bottles tell you to lather, rinse, and repeat? For the first time ever, I did. I almost did a third time, but my fingertips were so pruney, and my hair was so squeaky, that I was afraid I'd cut myself. Afterward, I pulled on my bathrobe and went downstairs. I microwaved a sausage biscuit, made it last as long as I could, and drank a tall glass of orange juice. Then I headed back upstairs for the moment of truth.

The sight of the blue suit at the far end of my closet made me sick. I know it sounds weird, but I really and truly got that sour throw-up taste in the back of my throat as soon as I laid eyes on it. What was the point? I cut my dad slack for a lot of things. But he had *no right* to wimp out like he was doing…and then guilt me into going anyway.

There was no getting out of it now.

I pulled on the suit pants and a button-down shirt, and I found a dark blue tie in the back of my sock drawer, and after three tries, I got it the right length. Then I slipped on the jacket. It felt like it weighed about a hundred pounds. I started to sweat, and for half a minute, I felt dizzy. But the feeling wore off, and I took a quick look in the bathroom mirror to make sure nothing about me was noticeable: I had that stiff look guys who don't wear suits get when they have to wear suits. Otherwise, I looked fine. I looked like I'd blend in with other guys in suits.

I ordered the Uber and trudged down the stairs.

Just as I got to the bottom, I heard the door to my dad's room creak open; I knew I'd woken him up, but I didn't care.

He called down to me, "You on your way to temple?"

"Yeah."

"You're a good son."

"Yeah."

I headed outside to wait for the Uber.

It arrived a couple of minutes later. When I swung open the back door, Winston was sitting at the far end of the seat. He had on a different white suit, a brighter white than the one he wore before, with a brighter white tie, and brighter white pants. The sun was streaming through the car windows and glaring off him; he was painful to look at, so I turned to the driver as I climbed inside.

"Flushing Synagogue?" the driver said.

"That's right."

Only after we'd been on the road for a few blocks did I glance over at Winston and mutter, "You're too white."

"You're looking pretty snazzy yourself," Winston said.

"You look like the Easter Bunny."

"Stroke of luck you're the only one who can see me."

"You dressed like the Easter Bunny for my sake?"

"I like to make a statement," he said.

"What statement is that? Happy Easter, Jews?"

"Ah, it's a laugh a minute with David Salmon!"

That made me smile. "Thanks for going with me."

"This whole religion thing, it's got me thinking."

"About what?" I asked.

"How would you feel about selling your soul?"

"Selling my soul? You've got to be kidding!"

"The thing of it is," he said, "my soul's cursed."

"How's that my problem?"

"The only way I can get it un-cursed is if I trade it for another...."

I stared at him in disbelief for like five seconds.

Then he started to crack up. "I had you going there, didn't I?"

"That's *not* funny."

But I was laughing, despite myself.

"Just trying to lighten the mood, Davey."

"You okay back there, kid?" the Uber driver asked, glancing back.

"Yeah, sorry, I'm okay. I just remembered an old joke."

"Don't be sorry, kid. Nothing wrong with an old joke."

I turned back to Winston and whispered, "I've got a question."

"Shoot."

"Why did you drag me to that cemetery last week?"

"I already told you—"

"No, what was the *real* reason?"

"Ah, you want the *real* reason."

"Yeah, I do."

"I like cemeteries," Winston said. "Always have."

"You don't think they're, you know, depressing?"

"Maybe, if you look at them a certain way. But I've always had a different view of 'em. Like when I pass by a line of graves, I think, 'Tee-hee, Grim Reaper got you and you and you, but I'm still here.'"

"Except…"

"Except what?"

"Except you're a hallucination. So, really, you're not here."

"That's a fair point," he said. "But whatever it is, here I am."

"I guess so."

"You should try it sometime."

"Try what?"

"Going alone to a cemetery. It can be downright uplifting."

"Except I did that last week," I said. "You were only there in my mind."

Winston chuckled. "Point taken."

The Free Synagogue of Flushing looks more like a courthouse than a temple, like the kind of place you're sent to find out if you're going to jail. It's a gigantic brick building at the top of a hill, surrounded by a shoulder-high brick wall that's topped with a spiked iron fence. The Uber dropped us off on the corner, and Winston and I stood and stared. It was a lot to take in. The only signs it was a temple were two twelve-foot-tall menorahs on either side of the main entrance and stained-glass windows that seemed to wrap around the building.

"It's only a couple of hours," I said, as much to myself as to him.

"You promise?"

We climbed up a dozen concrete stairs, then walked through a pair of tall oak doors, through a tiled waiting area, and into the temple itself. The place was huge. What you couldn't see from the street was that the ceiling was an enormous white dome with a stained-glass center. Sunlight was pouring in through it, and also through the stained-glass windows on all sides; the way the light was filling the place, you felt like there might be something to all the God and heaven and holiness stuff.

The two of us sat in the last pew. The rest of the congregation, maybe forty people, were crowded into the first ten rows, so there were at least twenty empty rows between us and everybody else.

Nothing much was going on yet. The service hadn't started, just lots of murmuring in the front rows. I turned to Winston, but he was staring straight up at the dome. He looked hypnotized by it, so I left him alone. I picked up one of the prayer books on the shelf in front of me and began to flip through it.

That was when a young guy, like twenty-five years old, with bushy black hair and a short black beard leaned into our row and handed me a black yarmulke.

"Oh, sorry," I said, and pressed it onto the back of my head.

"Maybe you'd like to move closer to the Torah, young man."

I looked up at him and smiled. "No, I'm all right here."

He smiled back. "Don't you want to get in on the action?"

The look on his face told me he wasn't going to let the thing drop, so I slid out of the row and followed him down front. Winston got there before I did. He was sitting two rows behind the last occupied row; I slid in next to him. The young guy wanted me to sit even closer, but I shook my head. I wasn't moving again. He gave me a quick shrug and headed up to the podium.

As he slipped on a prayer shawl, I realized he was the rabbi.

The service started, and Winston leaned back and folded his arms across his chest. That lasted for the first few minutes until the rabbi announced the *Shema*, which was the big prayer. The congregation rose to their feet, and Winston and I got up too. Then everybody started to sing: "*Shema Yisrael Adonai Eloheinu…*"

"I know this one!" Winston said.

"What?"

He sang, "*I flushed a snail, had to buy Liquid Drano….*"

"C'mon," I whispered, "that's disrespectful!"

"Says who?"

"I say so. It's just…disrespectful."

Except then I heard the words again in my head and cracked up. I couldn't help it; I snorted. The sound carried over the empty rows in front of us, and two old women turned and gave me hard looks. I tilted my head down until my chin was on my chest and fought back another laugh.

The *Shema* was the highlight of the service. Once it got said, and everybody sat back down in their seats, the service got pretty dull pretty fast. The rabbi had been going at it for forty-five minutes, and I was struggling to keep my eyes open, when Winston slid across the bench to get closer to me.

"So here's the deal, Davey. I've figured out the message."

"What do you mean?" I whispered.

"I've figured out the message you need to get to the Walrus."

"What's the message?"

"*Make it better*," he said.

"Make what better?"

"That, I don't know."

"Is that the whole message?"

"Yeah: *Make it better*."

"I guess it's easy enough to remember," I said.

He smiled and slid back across the bench.

"Wait," I whispered. "Who's the Walrus?"

"I don't quite know that either."

"Then how am I supposed to—"

"I know how to find him," Winston said.

"Good! Where is he?"

"Kennedy Airport."

"That's just great," I said. "Do you know how huge Kennedy Airport is?"

"He's not *at* the airport. He's near it."

"Where?"

"In a house."

"What house?"

He shut his eyes real tight, then opened them: "165-19 144th Avenue."

"C'mon. Did you just make that up?"

"No, that's the address," he said.

I pulled out my phone and emailed the address to myself. "Got it."

"Clever thingamabob."

"So that's where the Walrus lives?"

"He doesn't *live* there," Winston said. "But he's going to *be* there."

"When?"

"Wednesday night."

"*This* Wednesday?"

"Yeah."

"For how long?" I asked.

"Just Wednesday night. He moves around a lot. For a walrus, I mean."

"You're saying I've got to get to that house on Wednesday night?"

"That's the long and the short of it," he said.

"Do I just ring the doorbell and ask for the Walrus?"

"Davey boy, you're going to have to figure that one out by yourself."

Might as Well be Dead

My dad was sitting on the stoop in front of the house when the Uber dropped me off. He gave me a sad smile when he saw me get out of the car and patted the stoop next to him; he wanted me to sit down. It was one o'clock. I was starved, and I was dying to change into regular clothes, but the expression on his face told me there was no way I was going inside without talking to him first.

I sat down.

"Look at how grown up you are," he said. "I hardly recognized you."

"It's the suit."

"How'd you make out?"

"It was a good service," I said. "I got bored, but I stayed to the end."

"Did you say the prayers?"

"I guess...a few of them."

"You and I got to talk turkey, all right?"

"All right."

"I know I'm messing up," he said.

"Messing up what?"

He turned his head away from me, then turned back. "Being your father."

"C'mon!"

"Look, when your mom was here, I had one job. Bring home the bacon. That was it. I didn't have to worry about anything else. You mom took care of the rest of it. I had to bring home the bacon."

I started to laugh but caught myself. "Sorry."

Might as Well be Dead

He turned to me and smiled. "What's funny?"

"First, we're talking turkey, and now, we're talking bacon. It sounds like we're making a club sandwich."

He wiped a tear from his eye. "You're a strange kid."

"Anyway," I said, "you're not messing up anything."

"We both know the truth, David. I'm messing up."

"Even so, we'll get through it. You'll figure it out."

"Except what if I don't?" he said.

"I don't get what you're saying."

"What I'm saying is that you can count on me for some things, but not—"

I stood up. "Let's drop it, all right?"

He grabbed my hand and pulled me back down. "No, it's got to be said."

"*Why* does it have to be said?"

"Because down the line, I'm telling you, you may have to cut me loose."

"I don't even know what that means, *cut you loose*."

"It means that, down the line, when you're old enough to look out for yourself, I don't want you to worry about looking out for me too. Kids shouldn't have to look out for their parents."

I rolled my eyes. "Fine, I won't look out for you."

"Don't shrug it off, David. I'm being serious here. I'm damaged goods. I get up every morning hoping it's going to wear off, but it's not wearing off. You've got to take that into account when you think about your future."

"Fine, I'll take it into account."

"I just always figured your mom—"

That was as much as he could get out before the sobbing started. I slid closer to him on the stoop because

Might as Well be Dead

it felt like the right thing to do, and I thought about hugging him, but I didn't. I was afraid, if I did, it would prove his point. It would feel like I was looking out for him. Plus, neither of us was a hugger. It wouldn't feel natural.

After a minute like that, I said, "Do you mind if I change my clothes?"

He wiped his eyes on his sleeve. "You do whatever you need to do."

I stood up and headed into the house.

The talk with my dad stuck with me the rest of Saturday, and I was still replaying it in my mind after I woke up Sunday morning. Really and truly, it depressed the crap out of me. I felt bad for the guy, but the more I thought about it, the more annoyed I got. *Down the line, I might have to cut him loose*? How do you cut loose your dad? What was the point of even saying that? I had to fight off the urge to call my mom. I knew she'd be even more annoyed than I was, and then I'd get annoyed at her for being annoyed at him, since she was the one who'd left, and what purpose would my being annoyed at both of them serve?

So I just sucked it up.

I tried to concentrate on the one good thing that had come from dragging myself to temple: now at last I knew where to find the Walrus, and what message I was supposed to deliver. *Make it better*. Nothing complicated. I must have said those three words a hundred times under my breath. I tried different stresses: *Make* it better. Make *it* better. Make it *better*. I also tried no stress, which sounded more natural.

Make it better.

By dinner time on Sunday, the low feelings had started to lift, and I wasn't worrying as much about that conversation on the stoop. My dad was sitting on the couch, watching a football game, and he was leaning forward whenever the ball was hiked, and you could tell he cared about who was winning and losing. Which meant he wasn't feeling as low either, like he'd gotten off his chest what he needed to, and now he could make it through another Sunday night.

I sat down beside him on the couch; he nodded but kept his eyes on the TV.

"The Giants got this one in the bag," he said. "You want to eat out or call in?"

"Call in."

"What are you tasting?"

"How about a hamburger from the diner?" I said.

"Sounds good to me."

He grabbed his phone from the coffee table and placed the order, glancing up every few seconds at the TV. The football game ended about a few minutes later. That was when he turned to me, put up his right hand, and said, "God as my witness, Davey, I meant to go with you to temple. I wouldn't have brought it up otherwise. I wouldn't have made you go alone."

"Just don't expect me to go alone again," I said.

"I swear. Either both of us go, or neither of us."

Might as Well be Dead

I went to bed at nine o'clock on Sunday night and slept straight through till Monday morning. It was one of those dead-to-the-world sleeps, where you wake up in the same position you lie down, and it feels like only a minute has passed, and you can't remember a single dream. I hadn't slept like that in a *long* time, and as soon as I opened my eyes, I was in a good mood. The water in the shower felt the right temperature the second I stepped under it; I didn't have to adjust it a notch hotter or colder. The frozen waffles I toasted for breakfast tasted great without syrup. Even the orange juice had a sweet, fresh taste, and I *knew* the carton had been in the refrigerator for a least a week.

It was just a good Monday morning.

I glanced in both directions for Winston when I got outside, but once I put in my ear buds and started to walk, I forgot about him. The sun was right in my face, and it felt good too, especially with the breeze coming up behind me. It was like a perfect balance of warm and cool.

Hector and Minnie were waiting for me at the fire hydrant. I was kind of shocked to see her there, though not in a bad way. I figured it meant that she'd been serious when she said we could still be friends. That would be less awkward than avoiding her. It also required less planning.

She nodded at me in a knowing way and squeezed my hand.

Hector said, as much to himself as to either of us, "New week, new world."

Minnie and I turned to him and shot him looks.

Then the three of us cracked up; it was the best moment of the morning.

School was school though, and that good feeling wore off once classes started. Since Hector could take his own notes again, I went back to daydreaming, and the teachers noticed.

Mrs. Voros called me out during first period English. "Mr. Salmon, would you like to repeat the last thing I said?"

I looked up at her when I heard her call my name. "I'd rather not."

"What a Bartleby-like thing to say!"

"Who?" I asked.

The class laughed, and I shrugged.

"Bartleby is the main character in the story we're discussing," Mrs. Voros said.

"Oh."

"The narrator keeps assigning him tasks, and he keeps turning them down."

"Oh."

"Bartleby says that he prefers not to."

"Not to what?"

"Do you know the narrator's name?"

"No."

"That good because the narrator doesn't have a name. He's just the narrator."

"But he must have a name," I said.

"He doesn't...and of course you would know that if you had read the story."

"But *in real life*, he must have a name."

"He doesn't exist in real life, David. He exists in the story, and he has no name."

"That's pretty crappy," I said.

The class laughed again, but this time it felt like they were on my side, even though I wasn't exactly joking.

"Why is it crappy, David?"

"How come his parents didn't give him a name?"

"That's not a real question."

I began to choke up at that point, though only for a couple of seconds; it probably sounded more like coughing than choking, so nobody could tell. But I was definitely choking. Not because I gave a rat's butt about whether the guy in the story had a name, but because I realized I was *arguing* with Mrs. Voros in front of the class...and because, well, I didn't give a rat's butt about the thing we were arguing about.

I said, "How much trouble would it be for his parents to name him?"

"*He doesn't have par*—" She cut herself off before she got more upset. "David, he's a fictional character in a story by the American author, Herman Melville. Melville didn't give him a name, so we call him 'the narrator.' I'm sure, if he could step out of the pages of the story, he would have a name. But he can't step out of the pages of the story, so we simply don't know his name. Does that answer your question?"

"I guess," I said.

Might as Well be Dead

Lunch period started off real quiet because the cafeteria was serving lasagna, which was kind of the specialty of the house. It was the one time you felt like you were in an actual restaurant, the one time you felt bad for the gluten-free kids with their bagged lunches. The cafeteria ladies had big smiles on their faces as they dished it out, and nobody talked much when they got back to their tables. The focus, for once, was on the food.

I think there was an even split between those who wolfed it down and those who made it last as long as possible. Hector and Angela were make-it-last types; I was more of a wolf, though not a crazy, don't-stop-to-breathe wolf. I took sips of juice between bites; it's just that I took large bites. I got finished before they did. Afterward, I sat and didn't talk. I wanted to let them eat in peace.

It was interesting to watch them. Angela ate every last bite of her salad, and then her hard roll, before she started the lasagna. It was like she wanted a pure lasagna experience. Hector was the opposite. He kept going around his tray clockwise, salad then lasagna then roll. He never took two bites in a row of the same thing.

That was what I was doing, watching them, trying not to stare, when I felt somebody walk up behind me. It didn't feel unusual at first; it felt like somebody squeezing between the lunch tables. But whoever it was stopped and stood there. That made me crane my neck around. It was a guy I recognized but didn't know; he was in a couple of my classes, but I'd never said a word to him and had no idea what his name was. He was short, with a beefy pink face and red hair.

He didn't notice me noticing him. He was eyeing Hector.

Hector, meanwhile, was still focused on his lasagna.

Finally, the guy tapped Hector on the shoulder. "Hey."

Hector turned around and smiled up at him. "Yeah?"

The guy nodded at Angela. "Is that your fag hag?"

I heard the words, and I knew what they meant, and I thought: *What am I doing?* But by then I was already doing it. I remember turning and jumping to my feet, but I don't remember grabbing the guy, or the guy grabbing me back. I also don't remember how we got from the narrow aisle between the two lunch tables to the open area in front of the recycling bins. The next thing I knew, I had him in a tight headlock, and he had me by the waist, and we were spinning around and around. That was all we were doing, spinning around. Neither of us was punching or kicking. I could hear lots of yelling, and I felt a crowd surrounding us. But I couldn't see much. My eyes were open, but nothing was registering.

After about the sixth spin, the guy tripped and fell. He landed on his back, and I rode him down and landed on top of him, but the force of the fall made me let go of the headlock. For a few seconds, we were wrestling on the floor, and then at once I felt a pair of long arms snake under my armpits and yank me off him. Before the other guy could stand up, I saw a security guard dive on top of him and hold him down.

Hector spun me around to face him. It took me a second to realize he'd been the one who pulled me up;

the only thought I had, as weird as it sounds, was I couldn't believe how strong he was.

"Are you out of your mind?" Hector said.

Before I could answer him, another security guard grabbed me from Hector and frog-marched me out of the cafeteria.

I sat alone in Mr. Ivan's office for a long time before Mr. Ivan showed up. As he came through the door, he was smiling. It was hard to read what that smile meant, but I doubted it was going to be good.

"Well, David, I don't think you're ready for the UFC."

"I guess I'm in trouble."

"You guess right," he said. "You want to tell me what that was about?"

"No."

"Are you sure about that? It might make a difference."

I didn't want to sound rude, so I thought for couple of seconds. "No."

"That's all right. I talked to the other guy. I know what it was about."

"Am I going to be suspended?"

"I'm afraid so," Mr. Ivan said.

"For how long?"

"The rest of the week."

"Do you have to tell my dad?"

"What do you think, David?"

I sighed. "You've already called him, and he's coming to pick me up."

Might as Well be Dead

"That's how it works," Mr. Ivan said.

"Did you tell him what it was about?"

"Yes."

"Thank you," I said.

"Why are you thanking me?"

"Because if he knows what it was about, he won't be as freaked out."

"Whether your father is freaked out is beside the point, David. So is whether you had a noble reason for doing what you did. The point is *you can't do what you did*. Is that clear to you?"

"Yes."

"When I spoke to your father, I mentioned the possibility of you getting…help."

"You mean therapy?"

"That's what I mean," Mr. Ivan said.

"What did he say?"

"He said he'd talk to you about it."

"But you didn't say I *had* to do it?"

"David, no one is going to force you to do anything that you don't want to do."

"All right," I said.

"Now, let's go wait for your dad in front of the main gate."

With that, Mr. Ivan stood up and led me out of his office.

"Can we talk about this later?" my dad said, as I climbed into the car.

"That's fine with me."

"The thing is, I've got to get back to work. But if you need to talk—"

"No, it can wait."

"Mr. Ivan told me you were sticking up for your buddy."

"Well, yeah," I said, "but it was still a dumb thing to do."

"If you knew that, then why—"

"I just snapped."

"Did you get hurt?" he said.

"No."

"Did the other kid get hurt?"

"No," I said.

"That's a relief."

"Yeah."

"But we still have to talk about the whole *snapped* thing."

"I know."

"Then it's a deal? We're going to talk about it tonight?"

"It's a deal."

He dropped me off at the house and drove back to work.

Hector rang the doorbell later that afternoon. I'd figured he was going to text after school, but I didn't expect to see him at the front door. He was shaking his head as I pulled the door open.

"What were you thinking, David?" he asked.
"If I were thinking, I wouldn't have done it."
"Then why?"
"C'mon, Hector. You heard what the guy said."
"If it doesn't bother me, why should it bother you?"
"You're saying it doesn't bother you?"
"Yes, that's what I'm saying," he said.
"Wait! What are we talking about?"
"Minnie told me that she told you."
"Told me what?"
"Oh, for God's sake, David! I'm gay!"
"Who cares?"
"Judging by today, I think you do."
I took a deep breath. "Do you want to come in or not?"
He came in and sat the couch. "This place is a mess."
"Yeah, it's my mom's stuff."
"I figured out that much."
"So how did that guy know you were…you know?"
Hector grinned at me. "You can say the word."
"Gay. That's the word. How did he know you were gay?"
"*That guy* has a name. It's Stuart. He's in our sixth period Art."
"How does Stuart know you're gay?"
"Because I mentioned it in class last Friday," Hector said.
"You said it out loud?"
"You were there! Mr. Albala was talking about the Mona Lisa, and I asked if da Vinci was gay, and Mr. Albala said he wasn't sure…and you have no idea what I'm talking about, do you?"

"No."
"I came out," he said.
"You did?"
"I came out, and you missed it."
"What did you say?" I asked.
"I said that, as a gay person, I wanted to know which artists were gay."
"Oh."
"You missed that."
"Yeah, I guess so."
"Well, *that's* why you should pay attention," he said.
"Why didn't you tell me that you were gay?"
He laughed. "I meant to, but I got cold feet."
"You didn't trust me?"
"Of course, I trusted you!" he said. "But I was still nervous because…because you're you. Because you're my best friend. Because you've got enough on your plate right now. Then, when I found out Minnie had told you, I figured it was a done deal. I guess I should have told you. But it was easier at that point to let it go."
"Why didn't you tell me that Minnie had told you?"
"I could ask you the same question."
"She made me swear not to tell you," I said.
He slapped his head. "Are we actually going to have this conversation?"
I smiled. "I guess not."
"Good."
"So are things between us…still the same?"
"Are you asking me if I *like* you?" he said.
"Yeah."

"Well, I might like you if you were gay, but you're not, so I don't."

"Then I guess things are still the same."

"I guess so," he said. "Do you want to shake hands, or should we hug it out?"

"We can hug if you want."

We stood up and hugged.

"Thank you," he whispered in my ear.

I stepped back. "For what?"

"For the incredibly stupid and pointless thing you did at lunch."

That cracked me up, which cracked him up.

"You're suspended, right?"

"For the rest of the week."

"I'll take good notes for you," he said.

My dad came home earlier than usual, a couple of minutes after six o'clock. I sat at the window in the living room and watched for him to drive up; I knew he'd want to finish the conversation we started in the car, and I knew there was no avoiding it, so I wanted to get it over with as soon as he got home.

He saw me sitting at the window as he pulled the car into the driveway. He shrugged at me before he got out of the car. While he fumbled for his keys, I took a step to open the door for him. But then I changed my mind. I moved from the window to the couch. That was where I was sitting when he came through the front door.

"Do you mind if I ask you a question?" he said.

"I don't mind."

"How many fights have you had in your life?"

"Counting this one?"

"Counting this one."

"One," I said.

"That's what I figured. So what's different?"

"I don't know."

"You think maybe it's your mom not being here? Because that's what I think."

"Even if it is, she's not coming back," I said.

He sat down on the couch next to me. "What's your opinion of that Mr. Ivan?"

"I like him."

"Well, he's real high on the therapy thing."

"I know," I said.

"You think that's the way we should go?"

"*You've* got a problem too."

"Don't you think I realize that, David?"

"I'm not going to therapy unless you go."

His eyes flashed. "Number one, I didn't get into a fight. Number two, you don't make the rules around here. I make the rules, and you follow them. That may not be fair, but that's the way it is."

"Then why do you keep telling me how you're messing up?"

As the words came out of my mouth, I realized I was yelling. That seemed to catch my dad off guard. Not what I'd said, but the fact that I'd yelled at him. He leaned away from me and folded his hands in his lap.

He said, "Do you *want* me to go to therapy with you?"

"I don't want to go to therapy, period."

Might as Well be Dead

"Then you tell me, David. What am I supposed to do?"

"Why do you have to do anything? Why does either of us? I'm suspended for the rest of the week. I'll go back to school on Monday, and I'll be fine after that. I'll concentrate, and I'll get good grades. I promise."

"You're telling me I should…what?"

"Not make a big deal out of it."

"I don't want to make a big deal out of it," he said. "But it feels like *something* should happen."

"Do you want to punish me?"

"What would be the point of that? You know what you did was wrong, right?"

"Yeah, and stupid too."

"You're not going to do it again."

"Definitely not," I said.

"Okay then. Are we done here?"

"I think so."

He slapped his hands onto his knees, got up from the couch, and headed upstairs.

As I was climbing into bed, I got a two-word text from a number I didn't recognize: "Thank you."

"Who is this?" I wrote back.

"Angela Nunzio. From lunch."

"How did you get my number?"

"From Minerva. I asked her for it. I hope you don't mind."

"I don't mind. But what are you thanking me for?"

"For sticking up for me," she wrote.

I started to tell her that I was sticking up for Hector, not for her, but I caught myself and backspaced. Instead, I texted back, "You're welcome."

"Did you get hurt?"

"Just suspended."

"For how long?"

"Until the end of the week," I wrote.

"Do you need a note-taker?"

"You're not in any of my classes."

"But I have friends who are. I could ask them to take notes for you."

"Hector's going to take notes for me."

"What if Hector gets sick?" she wrote.

"If he does, I'll figure out something."

"Are you upset with me, David?"

"No!"

"I thought you might be upset since I was sitting at your table, and that's what started it."

"I'm not upset with you, Angela. I swear."

"What are you going to do with the week off?"

"I've got a couple of things lined up," I wrote.

Tuesday morning began with a call from Minnie. I was still in bed, but wide awake, when the phone rang. My neck cracked as I stretched over and picked it up before it rang a second time.

"It's me, David."

"Yeah, I know."

"Do you mind that I called?"

Might as Well be Dead

"No," I said.

"I thought maybe, since we're not a couple anymore, you might feel bad if I called."

"I don't feel bad. I'm fine."

She laughed. "You know, you could *pretend* to feel a little bad. Even if it's not true."

"Why would I do that?"

"For my sake. For the sake of my ego."

"I'm glad we're still friends. Does that help?"

She laughed again. "Maybe. *Slightly*."

"So why did you call me?" I asked.

"Angela told me what happened."

"Oh."

"You sound disappointed," she said.

"I'm just kind of sick of the subject."

"Well, you know I don't approve of fighting. But that was a rotten thing that boy said. You're a very loyal person, David, and Hector is lucky you're his friend. That's all I wanted to say."

"I guess."

"You *guess*?" she said. "Do you see? That's what I mean. It's just…it's so hard to picture you getting worked up about something. Right now, I can't picture you actually fighting. I'm trying to picture it in my head, and I can't. I can picture a guy who looks like you doing it, but I can't picture *you* doing it. I can't picture the expression you'd have on your face. Does that make sense?"

"I—"

"If you say, 'I guess,' I'm going to hang up."

"I don't know what to say."

"I'm talking about *passion*, David. It's the reason we broke up."

"I'm sorry?"

"Are you *asking* me if you're sorry or *telling* me you're sorry?"

"I'm sorry I'm not who you want me to be," I said.

"Are you being sarcastic?"

"No! If I could be a different way, I'd be a different way."

"Are you saying that you're unhappy with who you are?"

"No!"

"Then why—"

"I don't know," I answered. "I just want to say the right thing."

I could hear her choking up. "I've got to get dressed, David."

"All right."

"Can we maybe talk more about this?" she said.

"When?"

"I don't know. Maybe next week, when you're back in school."

"All right."

She hung up.

I put the phone back on the nightstand and rolled out of bed.

I was still lazying around my room a half hour later when my dad poked his head in and said, "How'd you like to come to work with me today?"

I thought about it for a couple of seconds. There wasn't much to do there, but I loved the smell of the place, and the hissing sound the steam press made. "Could I work the steam press?"

"David, you know I can't let you do that," he said. "There's no possible way."

"Why not?"

"If you burned yourself, I'd be out of business. I'd never get insured again."

"What about the conveyor?"

"If you run the conveyor, what's Max supposed to do?"

"He can take the money."

"It's not enough work for him. You don't need two people to do those jobs."

"Then I'll pass," I said.

"What are you going to do?"

"Hang around here, probably. I've got leftover homework."

He tapped the edge of the door twice, then walked out and slid it shut behind him.

I climbed back into bed and tried to fall to sleep, but I was still awake when I heard him leave the house, so I headed downstairs. I found Winston sitting at the kitchen table, smiling at me.

"What adventures await us today, Squire Salmon?"

"I was thinking about giving the cemetery another shot."

"Do tell!"

"That thing you said, about how it's not depressing if you look at it the right way."

"Right then! When do we leave?"

"No, I'm going alone."

"Ah!"

"No offense," I said.

"Man's got to do what a man's got to do. Hip hip and soldier on, my boy."

It took me a half hour to get out of the house, and then another half hour to walk to the cemetery. I was standing outside the gates, squinting into the morning sky, trying to get my mind right. *You're alive*, I told myself. *That's the thing to remember, the feeling Winston was talking about, the point of being here.* I walked through the gates and looked over the first rows of graves. Those headstones and monuments, each one of them stood for a life, a real life, as real as mine. They'd had their turn on top, their turn to squint at the sky, and now it was my turn. There was nothing bad about realizing that, about letting the thought wash over you, about being glad that your time was now.

That was what I was thinking as I wandered along the first of the winding paths.

You know what? Winston was right. It *wasn't* a sad place if you thought about it like that. It was just the opposite. Weaving around and between graves, knowing what you were walking over, what was underneath you, thinking about living and dying—it smalled up whatever you were going through. I got suspended from school for a few days. So what? Minnie broke up with me. So what?

Might as Well be Dead

I was alive. Those dead people buried in the ground, what would any of them have given to trade places? You think they wouldn't have shrugged off my troubles? You think they wouldn't have danced on their own graves for the chance?

So, yeah, Winston was right. But I was right too, at least about the mausoleum. It was one thing to stroll around outside among the graves, but it was a different thing to walk into the mausoleum. I thought about doing it on the way out of the cemetery; the door to the place was next to the exit, and it was wedged open. It was like an invitation. I even took a few steps in the direction of the door. But then I stopped and sat down on a concrete bench about ten steps away. Sitting there, I could see through the open door. I could see into the main room, where the tombs were...and I could barely breathe, that's how wrong I felt. The sight of the outside of the building, the rough stone walls, and then that narrow glimpse into the inside, with the sunlight glinting off the polished marble wall—it was like I could feel the weight of each casket behind that wall. It was like the weight of the entire place, the stone outside and the marble inside, was pressing down on my chest, and I really and truly couldn't breathe.

Let me tell you, I didn't sit there for very long.

I hurried out of the cemetery and didn't stop hurrying until I got to the donut shop on Northern Boulevard eight blocks away. I was still breathing hard as I sucked down a vanilla shake.

Even with how it ended, I counted the visit to the cemetery as a win. It felt as if I'd conquered it. From now on, it was a place I could go when I wanted to be by myself, and there weren't many places like that in my life. I was feeling pretty good as I started the long walk home.

Winston was waiting for me at the edge of Kissena Park. He was leaning up against a green metal signpost for the Q65 bus, tapping his foot on the sidewalk, glancing at his wrist as if he were wearing a watch, even though he wasn't. "What did I tell you?" he called.

"You were right."

"Lovely way to spend a morning, isn't it?"

"It was pretty good," I said.

"Gets the juices flowing."

"What juices?"

"The lifeblood! The very essence of being!"

"I only said it was pretty good."

"Makes you feel like you're up in it," he said. "Right in the thick of the thin."

"What do you want to do now?"

"Let life happen, son! Kick back and let it happen!"

"But *right now*," I said, "what do you want to do? Where do you want to go?"

"Are you hungry then?"

"I had a vanilla shake."

"Maybe we should reconnoiter," he said.

"What does that mean?"

"Go to the house. Get the lay of the land."

"You mean by Kennedy Airport?"

He nodded.

I shook my head. "There's no way I'm making *two* trips out there."

"Why not?"

"My dad checks his credit card bills," I said. "Don't you think he's going to count the Uber charges? We already rode to the temple and back, and tomorrow we have to ride out to deliver the message to the Walrus. Have you ever gone to the airport? That's a *long* trip. It's going to cost fifty dollars, at least, each way. I'm not going to do it twice. I'm not going to lie to him more than I have to. It's not worth it."

"That's a fair point," Winston said. "What, then?"

"I don't want to just stand here, on this corner."

He glanced in the direction of my house, and then in the opposite direction, toward Northern Boulevard. "What say we split the difference?"

With that, he pushed off the signpost and headed into Kissena Park. I followed him a couple of steps behind. He was walking fast, so I had to trot to catch up. By the time I did, we were walking past a playground. There were three moms sitting together on a green bench, chatting. Their kids were like three years old, two boys and a girl. They were doing what little kids do, running out of control and screaming at one another. As we passed by, the little girl tripped and fell. It was a cute thing to watch. The ground was padded, so she bounced right back up. But then she looked over at her mom—like she needed a signal to figure out if she was hurt. But her mom was chatting away, barely paying attention. The girl dusted off her pink pants and started running after the boys again.

Might as Well be Dead

We headed farther into the park, down a concrete path, until we got to Kissena Lake. Winston stopped there. There was a black metal rail at the edge of the water that came up to his chest. He wrapped his hands around the top bar and bent over. For a second, I thought he was going to vault over the thing and into the lake. Instead, he arched his back and stretched. It was a cat-like stretch, and he did it real slow. When he straightened up, I came to the rail beside him. We both stared out across the water. It wasn't much of a lake. You could throw a baseball from one side to the other.

It felt like a good time not to talk. Neither of us did; we only stood at the rail, side by side. But not talking gets boring pretty fast, so after a minute, I bent down, picked up a flat rock, and skimmed it across the lake. It skipped three times on the surface of the water; I thought it might make it to the grass on the other side, but after the third skip, it plunked in.

"Not a bad effort," Winston said.

I was glad he broke the silence.

He smiled. "Try another, then?"

I looked down. "That was the only flat rock."

"What about the one behind you?"

"That's too round. It won't skim."

"Never know till you try," he said.

I picked up the rock and tried to skim it. The second it hit the water, it sank.

"Told you," I said, smiling at him.

"Which would you rather be?"

"Which what?"

"Which stone."

"What do you mean, which stone?"

"Would you rather be like the first stone, skimming on the surface, or like the second stone, diving straight in?"

I started to laugh. "Is that supposed to be deep?"

"You seem like a regular skimmer to me," he said.

"If you say so."

"Nothing against it, mind you."

I looked him right in the eye, then heard myself say, "You're a swine."

That cracked up both of us. We stood at the rail and laughed until we were out of breath. Toward the end, Winston reached out and tugged on my shoulder. I felt closer to him at the moment than I ever had before.

"There's a question that's been nagging at me," I said.

"Shoot!"

"You're a hallucination, right?"

"That's *your* opinion."

"Except you *are*," I said. "That's the truth of it, isn't it?"

"I admit nothing!"

"No, but you are!"

His eyes got harder. "What are you getting at, David?"

"If you're in my head, you only know what I know."

He nodded once. "It follows like day follows night."

"Then how do I know where the Walrus is going to be tomorrow?"

"Ah!"

"Well?"

"You're on the tusks of a dilemma. That's for sure."

"Tusks?"

"Walrus, remember?"

"Getting back to my point: *Is* the Walrus going to be at that house?"

"Hmm…"

"Does the Walrus even exist?"

"Seems to me there's only one way to find out," Winston said.

I couldn't argue with that.

He leaned in closer. "You have something else on your mind."

"Yeah, I do. But it's…hard."

"Just spit it out."

"What happens next?"

"How do you mean?"

"After tomorrow," I said.

"The day after tomorrow happens after tomorrow."

"No, let's say that there *is* a Walrus, and he's at that house, and I deliver the message to him. What happens after that?"

"Well, Davey, I'm not quite sure."

"You're still going to hang around, right?"

"It's possible, I suppose."

"I know I've said mean things to you…"

"Let's have none of that, young knight!"

"I thought I was a squire."

"You're due a promotion."

"But you're not going to just evaporate, right?"

He shrugged. "Your guess is as good as mine."

Hector started to text me classroom notes as soon as school let out. He must have sent them from his laptop while he was riding home on the bus, which figured since he took notes on his laptop. You should have seen them! Chunky paragraphs with bullet points and even a few illustrations he'd pulled off the internet. He also highlighted each page—yellow, if he thought the information was interesting, blue if he thought it was crucial, and red if he was sure it was going to be on the next test. (He had a color code at the bottom of the first page, so I knew what each one meant.) Page after page, the notes came, and by the end he'd sent me sixteen pages.

Sixteen pages of notes from one day of classes!

When the bombardment was over, I thanked him and went back to lying in bed with my eyes shut. I did that for a couple of hours. What shocked me was how hard it was to fill up an entire afternoon when you're not in school, but you're not home sick. When you're just…home. There's only so much TV and YouTube you can watch.

The one thing that kept me going, the one thing that took my mind off the boredom, was the thought that I was going to meet the Walrus the next day. Or else I was going to show up at a stranger's house, ask a question that made no sense to whoever was home, and get the door slammed in my face. If I got the door slammed in my face, that proved I was crazy. On the other hand, if it turned out that there actually was a guy called the Walrus inside, and I delivered the message, *that proved I was even crazier*. Because that meant that I knew stuff I didn't know I knew. It meant I had information, but I had no idea how it got into my head.

That was a scary thought.

Angela texted as I was looking out the window at the sunset. "How did your first day of suspension go?"

It seemed weird that she would text me again, but I was glad for the distraction. "It went all right."

"Did you do anything fun?"

"Went to the park. Skimmed rocks."

"Which park?"

"Kissena," I wrote back.

"Really? I don't live far too from there."

"Where do you live?"

"On 73rd Avenue, by Utopia Parkway."

"That's nowhere near Kissena Park."

"But it's not too far. I could go there."

"Isn't there a playground on your block?" I wrote.

"Utopia Playground. Do you know it?"

"I played baseball there a few times."

"I take tennis lessons there," she texted. "Maybe we were there at the same time."

"I guess it's possible."

"It's too bad," she wrote.

"What's too bad?"

"That we didn't say hello."

"How could we say hello if we'd never met?"

"I guess you're right. But it's still fun to think about, isn't it? How your life crosses with other people's lives. Don't you think that's fun to think about? How many strangers you pass every day, and each one of them has a story."

"But you don't know them."

"But you could know them," she wrote. "You could meet them later on, and they could turn out to be amazing, and then you figure out you could have met them way before you met them."

I put down the phone on the nightstand and stared at it for a half minute.

"Still there?" Angela texted.

"Yes."

"Did I get too personal?"

"No, but I didn't think you liked to text so much."

"I like texting because it's exact," she wrote. "Talking is much sloppier."

"Why do you say that?"

"When you're texting, you get to look over the words before you send them. You can make sure they're the right words. You don't have to hit send until you're sure. When you're talking, once the words come out of your mouth, they're gone."

"Except you can think about the words before you say them."

"What if the person walks away before you open your mouth?"

That cracked me up...since there was *no way* that could have occurred to her unless it had happened.

"Do you play tennis?" she wrote.

"I have a racket, but I don't play a lot."

"Maybe we could play at Utopia Park."

"When?"

"I don't know. Sometime. It gets crowded on the weekends. But after school it's not too bad, and there's still lots of daylight left. It's a little cold out, but if you wear a sweater, you don't feel it."

"That sounds good," I texted.

"When do you want to do it?"

"We can figure it out after I get back to school next week."

"You don't have to do it if you don't want to," she wrote.

"No, I want to do it. I just don't want to make plans now."

"I understand."

"I really and truly want to play tennis with you, Angela."

"I do too."

I waited for another message, but none came, so I lay back down and closed my eyes.

I came downstairs when my dad got home, and we ordered a pizza. He spent most of dinner apologizing that he couldn't let me work the steam press at the cleaners—which I hadn't even thought about since he'd said no that morning. He went on and on about how sorry he was; you could tell he'd been working on that apology the entire day. He had a long list of reasons he couldn't let a kid work the steam press, but he made sure to tell me, over and over, that he knew I was mature enough to handle it. I tried to listen, but most of the time he spent apologizing, I spent thinking about how weird life was, how the guy who says no winds up feeling bad, whereas the guy who asks winds up forgetting about the whole thing.

That was how life worked; it was just weird.

Since I'd slept so much during the day, I couldn't fall asleep that night. I kept turning on the TV, watching for a half hour, then turning it off to see if maybe boredom would put me to sleep. But no luck. I tried to imagine what the Walrus would look like; I kept picturing him as a fat guy with a droopy white mustache sitting on a couch. But what if "the Walrus" was just his nickname because his real name was Walter? Then he could look like a Walter, which meant he could look like anybody.

After midnight, I sat up in bed and thought about calling my mom. But what would be the point? If I told her about the Walrus, and the message I was supposed to deliver, and the place I had to go to deliver it, and the ride I had to take to get there, she'd worry herself sick. Plus, I couldn't call her after midnight.

I'd tell her about it after it had happened.

I went to the bathroom and washed my face. The warm water felt good on my skin, and the soap smelled like almonds. It was a calm, middle-of-the-night smell. It made me yawn, and I thought maybe I was ready to climb back in bed. But I changed my mind when I came out of the bathroom. I tiptoed downstairs and saw my dad asleep in the rocking chair. His feet were propped up on two of the boxes of my mom's stuff. His arms were curled tight across his chest, like he was cold. I grabbed a blanket from the couch and draped it over him. He half woke up when I did that; he smacked his lips twice, like he had a bad taste in his mouth, but then he pulled the blanket close and fell back asleep.

Wednesday morning, the earliest light of it, woke me up after maybe three hours of sleep. As soon as I opened my eyes, I was wide awake. Bone tired, but wide awake. My right hand was tingling, so I clenched and unclenched it until it felt normal. By then, there was no point in rolling over and trying to fall back asleep; it wasn't going to happen.

I dragged myself out of bed, and out of boredom I did a couple of the homework assignments Hector had sent along with his notes. That was what I was doing when my dad poked his head into the room.

He was smiling when I glanced over at him.

"What?" I asked.

"Remind me to tell you someday how I lucked out in the son department."

I nodded. "I will."

He nodded back at me and shut the door.

It took him another half hour to leave for work. He called goodbye as he headed out, and I answered him, and that was that. The house got suddenly quiet; I had it to myself. I knocked off one last algebra equation and came downstairs. Winston was sitting in the rocking chair, going back and forth. He'd wrapped himself in the blanket I put over my dad the night before, which bugged me. I was going to say something, but I realized that that was the reason he did it. To get a rise out of me. I was starting to get a feel for the guy, how his mind worked. I let the thing with the blanket go.

"What time do you want to leave?" I asked.

"Beats me, mate. That's your call."

"But the Walrus will be there tonight, right? *Tonight*."

"Meaning what?"

"He's not there now. He won't be there until tonight."

"If you say so."

"No, *you* said so. That's exactly what you told me."

He cracked a smile. "Had you going, didn't I?"

"What?"

"I'm pulling your leg, son. I'm funning with you."

I shook my head. "It's not funny. It's obnoxious"

"Now, now, Davey, let's not quarrel. Not today."

"Then just tell me what time we should leave."

"Five o'clock, I think."

"Fine," I said. "I'll text my dad that I'm going to Hector's house."

"Does he have Hector's number?"

"Not that I know of."

"Does he know Hector's last name?"

"No."

"Sounds foolproof…"

"C'mon, he's not going to check up on me," I said. "He trusts me."

As I said that, I felt a little stab in my heart: My dad *did* trust me.

"So you're golden," he said. "Just one problem. We're not going."

"What do you mean?"

"*We're* not going. *You're* going."

"I don't get it," I said.
"You're flying solo, my boy…."
I gasped but caught myself. "Why?"
"It's not my place to go with you."
"But how will I know the Walrus?"
"You'll have to ask," Winston said.
"Why are you doing this?"
"I just told you. It's not my place."
"Meaning what?"
"If it were my place, I could have delivered the message myself."
"Suppose I don't go unless you go?"
"If you don't go, then you don't go," he said. "Whatever it is, it is."

There was no possibility I wasn't going to go. It wasn't even a good bluff, but that was how we left it: *Whatever it is, it is.* I ate strawberry Pop Tarts for breakfast, then took a long walk around the neighborhood. While I was out, I reserved an Uber for five o'clock. I put in the address Winston had given me, and the fare came up as fifty-six dollars. Which meant that when my dad checked his credit card bill at the end of the month, he'd know for sure I hadn't gone to Hector's house…and I'd lied to him.

Morning bled into afternoon, and I kept walking. Eventually, I wound up on the 159th Street footbridge, staring down at the Long Island Expressway. It was a place that used to terrify me when I was a little kid. My mom would take me up there, and we'd watch the cars zoom by underneath us, and then I'd notice a truck in the distance, a huge eighteen-wheeler, and it would get closer and closer, and it looked like there was no way it could fit under the footbridge, and it was going to crash into it, and into us, and the two of us, me and my mom, were going to fly into the air, and then fall to our deaths on the highway below. And I would brace for it, for flying into the air, and then falling onto the highway. Except then the truck would rumble right underneath us, missing the footbridge by inches, or at least that's what it felt like, and the entire footbridge would shake, and my mom would lift me up and twirl me around.

Now, as I stood on the footbridge, and I saw a truck hurtling toward me, I couldn't have cared less. I knew it was going to miss. That's what growing up means. You know the truck is going to miss.

For lunch, I had a sausage sandwich at the Dunkin Donuts on Kissena Boulevard. It tasted sweeter than I remembered their sausage sandwiches tasting. I kept staring at it in my hand every time I took a bite, wondering how it could be that good. Even the Diet Coke seemed sweeter and flatter than usual, which was how I liked it.

I walked more after lunch, killing time. I headed over to Queens College and hiked around the campus. That was where my dad met my mom. They were both students; I knew the story because they used to razz one another about it. I knew the exact spot he had first talked to her. He'd chased her down on a triangle of grass next to the Student Union and struck up a conversation. I even knew what they'd talked about: a philosophy teacher they both hated. They weren't in the same class, but they had the same teacher. My dad saw my mom carrying the textbook from the class, and he ran after her and struck up a conversation. Just like that. He started a conversation. If she wasn't holding that textbook under her arm, I would never have gotten born.

It *was* weird to think about.

Angela was right about that.

Around three o'clock, I headed back home. I left myself enough time to wash up and put on clean clothes since I'd sweated with all the walking I did. As I was changing, Hector texted me another batch of notes. I didn't look at them; I waited until the last text came, and then I texted back, "Thanks." Afterward, I headed outside and sat on the stoop.

The Uber pulled up in front of the house at exactly five o'clock, and I climbed into the back seat.

"David?" the driver said.

"That's me."

He made a U-turn and headed for the highway.

The trip took an hour and a half. It should've gone a lot quicker, but we got caught in traffic on the Van Wyck Expressway. It was bumper to bumper. I tried not to worry about it. It wasn't like I was on a tight schedule. All I had to do was find a guy and deliver a message: *Make it better*. Whether I found him and delivered the message at six o'clock or seven o'clock made no difference to me.

The traffic got worse and worse as we got closer to the airport. We'd come to a stop and not move for a full minute. Horns would start to blare, and every so often, my Uber driver would honk his. Then he would mutter a curse under his breath; I think, if he'd had a grown up in the back seat, he would have yelled the curse out the window. I thought about telling him to go ahead and do it, to curse out the window if that was what he felt like doing, but I didn't want to embarrass him.

Twilight came into the car as we inched along. As the sky darkened, you could see the glow of lights from Manhattan to the west. It was far off. You couldn't make out the buildings, just a hazy glow. Within minutes, the headlights of the cars that were jockeying in and out of lanes behind us were playing across the back seat. The lights would reflect off the rearview mirror in the front seat and hit me in the eyes when I wasn't expecting them, and I would close my eyes. I began to feel slightly sick. Nothing too bad, just nausea. The back seat had a faint cigarette smell you didn't notice when the car was zipping along, but when it was crawling, you got a good whiff of it. I rolled down the window, but the exhaust from the cars on the highway was worse than the cigarette smell, so I rolled the window back up.

"You doing all right back there, my friend?"

"I'm all right," I said.

"Hang in there. Just one more exit."

"I'm fine."

"What's cooking in Rockaway?"

"What do you mean?"

He laughed. "Business or pleasure?"

"I'm doing a favor for a friend."

"Long ride to do a favor. Must be a good friend."

"He gets on my nerves sometimes," I said.

"Yeah, well, friends have a way of doing that."

The highway exit came in sight a couple of minutes later, and the driver cut across two lanes of traffic to angle for it. Cars were honking at us like crazy, but I didn't care. We hit the ramp and picked up speed, then drove in a tight loop, and wound up on something called the Belt Parkway. There was almost no traffic now. We got off the Belt Parkway after a few more minutes, and then we were back on regular streets.

Finally, the driver pulled over and said, "Here you go."

I looked in both directions. "Where's the house?"

He pointed. "That yellow one over there, three houses up the block, with the big guy standing out front. You can see the address under the porch light, 165-19. You want me to wait and make sure everything is copacetic?"

"No," I said. "You can go."

I got out of the car and waved as he drove off.

It was just a regular looking house, except for the big guy standing on the porch. He looked even bigger because the porch was three steps up from the front yard. The yard was jammed with flowering bushes; some of the flowers were hanging over and poking through the iron fence that surrounded the place. It looked like they were straining to get out, to take a walk around the neighborhood, to see what was what.

The big guy on the porch was a black guy. He had on a black baseball cap, a black T-shirt, and black plants. Even his shoes were black. He noticed me as I stopped in front of the house. He smiled at me. The smile lasted until I pushed open the gate and stepped into the front yard.

He shook his head. "Turn around, kid."

Lights were on inside the house, and lots of people were moving around. I couldn't see their faces, but I could see their shadows against the window shades. The shades were drawn on all the windows.

I took another couple of steps toward the front door.

The guy stepped off the porch and into the yard. "Kid, what did I just tell you?"

I smiled up at him. "I'm looking for the Walrus."

He started to laugh. "You and about half the population of the planet."

"I don't get it," I said.

"You think you're the only one looking for the Walrus?"

"Isn't he here?"

"How do you know who's here and who isn't here?"

"I don't even know who he is."

"Then why are you looking for him?" the big guy asked.

"I've got a message for him."

"Is that right?"

I nodded. "Yeah."

He rolled his eyes. "Go home, kid."

"No, you don't understand—"

That was as much as I got out before I started to gag. It came over me all of a sudden. My insides clenched up, starting in my guts and working up into my throat. I kept mouthing words, but nothing was coming out; I couldn't get any air behind them. I couldn't get air in or out. I started to cough.

The big guy stepped forward until he was right in front of me. He bent down so that we were eye to eye. He had a soft expression on his face. The longer I looked at him, the calmer I got.

"What's your name?" he said.

"David."

"David, what?"

"David Salmon. Like the fish."

He put out his hand, and I shook it.

"I'm Keith," he said.

"I'm David Salmon."

"So you said. Where do you live, David Salmon?"

"Flushing."

"You're lying!"

"It's the truth," I said.

"How'd you get here?"

"I took an Uber. My dad lets me."

"Your dad lets you take an Uber and show up at a stranger's house…at night?"

I turned my head. "No."

"Then what are you doing?"

"I just told you," I said. "I've got to see the Walrus. I've got a message for him."

"What's the message?"

I turned to face him again. "I can't tell you. I can only tell him."

He sighed. "How are you going to get home?"

"I guess I'll call another Uber."

"Suppose I let you in to see the Walrus. You promise to go home after that?"

"Yes."

"I'm going to have to pat you down first," he said. "Are you cool with that?"

"What does that mean?"

"I have to search you for weapons. You've never seen a pat-down on TV?"

"Oh, okay, I know what you mean."

I stretched my arms away from my body, and he patted me down. It only took a few seconds, even though he spun me around twice. It felt weird, not so much the pat down as the idea that he thought I might have a weapon. But it also felt kind of grown up. Grown-ups get patted down. Grown-ups take Ubers and get patted down.

"All right, David Salmon," he said. "You're clean."

"Now what?"

"Follow me."

He walked back up the steps onto the porch, and I followed him. When we reached the door, he knocked on it. Three quick knocks. Maybe five seconds passed, and then the door slid open. Not all the way, only a couple of feet. Behind the door was another big black guy dressed in black clothes.

I got excited when I saw him and blurted out, "Are you the Walrus?"

Keith glared back at me. "Shush!"

Might as Well be Dead

He and the other guy whispered back and forth for like half a minute. The other guy was shaking his head at first, but then, as they spoke, he began rubbing his chin with his left palm. Finally, he nodded. He nodded twice and went back into the house. He left the door open.

Keith grabbed me by the hand and led me through the door. He led me into a living room with maybe twenty-five people. To one side, there were two folding tables with food on them, lots of vegetables and dips, red and green grapes, and a couple of plates of cheese squares. On the other side of the room, on a third folding table, were drinks. Most of the people were drinking juices or bottled waters, but a few had plastic cups with red or white wine. There were also about a dozen guitars lying in open cases and pushed up against the back wall.

Nobody noticed us walk in. Keith sat me down on a wooden folding chair in the far corner of the room, next the bathroom.

"Now here's what's going to happen," he said. "You're going to sit here, and you're not going to do anything, or bother anybody, and you're going to wait for the Walrus to come out and say hello."

I nodded. "How long will it take?"

"Could be a few minutes. Could be longer. But however long it takes, you're going to sit here and fade into the background. Do we have a deal?"

"Yeah."

"Now I've got to go back outside."

"You can't stay?"

"I'm working, kid! I'm not partying!"

"But—"

Might as Well be Dead

"You'll be fine." He glanced over at the food tables. "You want something to eat?"

"No thanks," I said.

"Don't get me in trouble, all right?"

"I won't."

For the first couple of minutes, not much happened. I sat in the corner and looked around; I tried to take in the entire room. I kept my eyes out for the Walrus…which made no sense since I had no clue what he looked like. From where I was sitting, it was a bunch of random people mingling, laughing with one another, and going back and forth to the tables for food and drinks. If I had to guess their ages, I'd say most were in their forties. But they dressed younger. That was the thing that stood out. The guys were wearing tight pants and T-shirts with colorful, splashy designs; the women had on tight pants too, and sleeveless shirts or shirts that showed their belly buttons. It was just weird. I mean, my mom and dad were in their forties too, but I couldn't imagine either of them wearing clothes like that. The other thing I noticed was that pretty much all of them were thin. There were a couple of chunky guys with tattoos up and down their arms, but neither of them had a gut; they just looked strong. What were the chances that not one person in the room would be fat? There were no kids except me. That made me self-conscious. But nobody seemed to care or even pay attention. Every so often, somebody would duck into the bathroom and nod or smile at me, like you do when you pass somebody on your way to the bathroom, but that was about it. Otherwise, I felt invisible.

I'd been sitting there for maybe ten minutes when one of the guys broke away from the group he was chatting with and headed toward the wall of guitars. You knew, just from the way he looked, he was going to start playing one of them. He had straight black hair that came down the back of his neck and three earrings in one ear and long fingernails on his right hand but not his left. Sure enough, he bent over the first guitar, lifted it out of its case, and sat down on a wooden folding chair like mine. He gave the guitar a loud strum. As soon as he did that, people got quiet. They wandered over and formed a loose circle. I couldn't see him at that point. But I could hear him strumming the guitar.

Then he started to sing, and a second later the rest of them were singing with him. It took me a few more seconds to recognize the song, but when I did, it hit me hard. It was a Beatles song my mom used to sing to me when I was a little kid—when I was *real* little, like three years old. It was the earliest memory I had. It was a song about a guy who's writing a love letter to a girl. My mom would play the song on a record player, an actual going-round-and-round record player, and she'd sing along with it, and hold my hand, and dance me around the room, and then, whenever the big line came, "PS, I...love...you," she'd squat down, and sing it straight into my face, and then came "you, you, you," and she'd sing the words and poke me in the chest with her finger.

It got me real emotional, hearing that. I started to shake, and I felt a tear leak down my cheek, but I brushed it off before it got very far. I folded my hands in my lap and tried to look calm.

Then the guy started to sing another song, and again the rest of them joined in, and it got me going again, because it was another song from that Beatles record, the one my mom used to play. But it was a faster song. She used to dance to it as she vacuumed, and I'd sit on the floor and watch her. She'd push the vacuum cleaner forward and back, and she'd swivel her hips like she was hula-hooping, and she'd come right at me with the thing and dance circles around me, and it would feel like I was getting sucked up in the noise, and the dance, and the song. It was so clear in my head, the memory. It was like I could feel the suction of the vacuum cleaner at my feet.

Then the guy started a third song, and it was *another* song from that old Beatles record my mom loved, and by then I was getting even more emotional, because I knew life was never going to be like that again. It was never going to be that good again since we were never going to be a family again, not a real one, living in the same house. Those times were gone, and they were never coming back, and I was gagging again, and my insides were churning and clenching, and everybody was singing, and the words and music were curling around me, and I could barely breathe, that's how many feelings were going through me.

"Is there a David in the house?" a voice called.

The song stopped. The room got quiet.

I heard the words, and I was still gagging and shaking, but I got enough breath inside me to raise my hand.

The crowd separated, and an old man with dark hair and moist, droopy eyes came forward. His eyes zeroed in on me. "Are you David?"

I nodded. That was as much as I could do.

"I heard you're looking for me," he said.

I nodded again and stood up; my heart felt like it was going to crack open.

He smiled. "Something about a message?"

My breaths started to go rapid fire in and out of my mouth; I felt like I was vibrating, like there was no way I could speak. I closed my eyes and bore down. It took maybe ten seconds, but then I opened my eyes again and got out, "Are you the Walrus?"

That cracked up the entire room. The sound of their laughter washed over me, and my breaths began to slow down. I could hear my heart again. It was loud and fast, and it felt high in my chest, but at least I could hear it, and I could take normal breaths.

The old guy was smiling at me. "You're a cheeky one, aren't you?"

I wasn't sure what he meant, but I nodded. "*Are* you the Walrus?"

"That's the rumor."

I looked over at the guy with the guitar, then back at the Walrus.

"Are those your songs?"

"I wrote them, yeah" the Walrus said. "I guess they're mine."

"I have a message."

"Yes?"
"Make it better."
"Make what better?" he asked.
"I…I thought you'd know."

That got another big laugh from everybody, but the Walrus shushed them.

"You're not making sense, son."

I started to choke up again; I felt another tear leaking down my face, and another, and another after that one, but I didn't brush them away. *How could the Walrus not know what the message meant?*

"Now, now, none of that," the Walrus said. "You're all right, son. You're safe here. No one's going to hurt you."

"My mom…"
"Yes."
"My mom…"
"Yes."
"My mom…"
"Yes, I got that bit. Is your mom a fan of mine?"

I nodded.

"Could've been worse," the guy with the guitar shouted. "Could've been his grandmum."

That cracked up the crowd one more time.

"Do you want an autograph for your mum?" the Walrus said.

"No!"

More laughter, but again the Walrus shushed them. "What, then? Don't be afraid."

"My mom…"
"We're back on that, eh?"

Might as Well be Dead

"My mom..."
"Son—"
"My mom..."
"What about her?"
"She killed herself."

As soon as I heard the words come out of my mouth, the flood came. It was like a dam broke, and the entire world went underwater. Through the blur, I saw the Walrus step forward, and I felt him hugging me, and seconds later the dryness of his shirt began to soak up the wetness of my face.

I don't know how long the two of us stood like that, but it felt like a long time.

What happened next, I don't remember too well. I wound up in a back room with the Walrus and Keith, the guy who'd let me into the house. They were handing me tissues, and Keith kept pushing a bottle of water into my hand and telling me to drink. The Walrus was talking to me, and I was answering him; I can hear his voice clearly, right now, in my head, but I don't remember one thing he said. The main thing I remember is feeling embarrassed that I'd ruined their party.

I don't know how long I was in the back room. The next clear memory I have is Keith saying, "Tell me again where you live, David."

"Flushing."

"What's your address?"

I told him my address.

"I'm going to drive you home, okay?"

I nodded.

Keith handed me a fresh bottle of water and led me out of the back room. The people in the living room went quiet as we passed. I looked straight down; I didn't want to meet anybody's eyes. Six of them, or maybe more, reached out and ran their hands through my hair or grabbed me by a shoulder and squeezed.

I followed Keith out the front door and into the cool night air. He walked me through the yard and to the sidewalk, and he opened the rear door of a big black car. I climbed into the back seat, still clutching the bottle of water, and closed my eyes. He circled around the car, got into the driver's seat, and turned on the engine.

Then, for several minutes, we just sat there.

Finally, the rear door next to me swung open, and the Walrus said, "Scoot over."

I looked up at him, confused. "You're coming with us?"

"Only if you scoot over."

He smiled at me, and I scooted over.

He got in, shut the door, and tapped on the side window.

Then Keith started to drive.

I just stared out the side window. I was afraid, if I looked over, and the Walrus was looking back at me, I might start to bawl again. I figured I'd caused enough trouble; I didn't want to make things worse.

I began to relax once we got on the highway. I pushed the bottle of water into a side compartment on the door next to me, then leaned back into the seat. Out of the corner of my eye, I noticed that the Walrus was working on his cell phone, typing messages, and paying no attention to me.

That was when I looked up.

Winston was sitting in the front passenger seat, next to Keith, looking back at me. He put his finger up to his lips and said, "Shhh!"

I took a long breath, then blinked my eyes to let him know I understood.

"He's an old, estranged fiancé of mine," Winston said.

I wasn't sure what he meant; I peeked over at the Walrus, then cocked my head to the side.

Winston laughed. "Hard to believe, isn't it? He wasn't always a geezer though. You wouldn't know it to look at him, but he had a real pretty face. The birds were mad for him. You should've heard them scream. I used to tease him about it, how the birds were always screaming his name. It got under his skin since he thought I was saying something against him. That's why I did it—because I knew it got under his skin. But he was my mate, and I loved him, and nothing in the world is more final than your mates. Whatever else comes and goes, in the end, you've got your mates."

Winston glanced over at the Walrus, then back at me.

"Look at him, tap-tap-tapping away! Hasn't got a clue!"

I shrugged.

Then Winston's face lit up. "I've got an idea. You game?"

I nodded.

"Now I want you to say out loud, after me: *I'm getting better.*"

"I'm getting better," I said.

The Walrus peered at me and smiled. "Today was a big day."

Then Winston said, "Now say: *I'm getting better all the time.*"

"I'm getting better all the time," I said.

"That's the spirit, son. Darkest before the dawn and all that."

Winston shook his head. "The daft git…he still doesn't get it!"

"Get what?" I muttered.

"Come again?" the Walrus said.

"Now say this, just like I say it," Winston said. "*Getting so much better all the time.*"

"Getting so much better all the time."

The expression on the Walrus's face changed. His eyes focused in on mine, and a look came into them like he'd just gotten the last word of a crossword puzzle, but he didn't quite trust the answer. He said, more like a question than an answer, "Can't get much worse…."

I felt a smile come across my face. "I guess I *can't* get much worse, can I?"

Then, for no reason I could figure out, the Walrus began to laugh, and a second later Winston began to laugh. The two of them were having a quiet laugh, not quite together, except in my mind, but at the same time, so it felt like both of them were in on the same joke. Maybe they were laughing at what I'd said, or at something else, or at one another. I had no idea. But the sound of their voices, laughing at the same time, filled my ears, and my head, and my heart.

You should have seen the look on my dad's face when he opened the door, and I was standing on the stoop next to the Walrus. His eyes got as big as grapes, and his mouth fell open. It was like he'd been hit by lightning, like you could have stuck a light bulb in his mouth, and it would have lit up, or maybe even exploded. You could see him struggling to get a word out, but he couldn't do it.

"Your boy turned up on my tour," the Walrus said, smiling. "I'm returning him for the deposit."

"Thank you," my dad sputtered.

"Can I come in then?"

My dad blinked hard, then said, "Yes. Yes. Definitely."

The Walrus and I walked into the living room, and my dad followed a step behind. I got embarrassed by the boxes of my mom's stuff strewn on the floor, but only for a second. On the list of things to feel embarrassed about right then, the fact that our living room was a mess seemed pretty low.

My dad snatched his sports jacket off the couch and said, "Please, sit down."

The Walrus and I sat down on the couch, and my dad sat down on the edge of the ottoman. He was still wearing his work shirt, and he loosened his tie. It seemed like a strange thing to do, but I guess he was still having trouble catching his breath.

"I'm sorry for your loss," the Walrus said.

"How do you…?" My dad cut himself off, then said, "Thank you."

The Walrus turned to me at that point and said, "Would you mind if your dad and I talked in private?"

"I don't mind."

I headed upstairs to my bedroom and left them alone. Winston was sitting on the edge of my bed, waiting for me, like I thought he would be.

"What do you figure those two are on about?" he asked.

"I guess they're talking about how I need help."

"You do, you know."

"Yeah, I know," I said.

"What were you thinking, running off like that?"

"You're the one—"

"I'm a figment of your imagination, remember?"

"But you're my friend. You just said—"

"Ah, Davey! What are we going to do with you?"

"You think I need therapy?"

"Oh, at the very least," Winston said, nodding.

"I guess…if I have to."

"I wouldn't rule out that temple thing either."

"C'mon!"

"You and your dad together. Be good for you."

"Since when—?"

"Haven't you noticed I'm a sucker for chants?"

"You'll come with us, right?"

He sighed. "You know the answer to that, son."

"No!"

"Now we'll have none of that, David Salmon!"

I started to tear up. "Why does getting better mean you have to go?"

He leaned in till our faces were close. "Boy, there *is* worse to come."

"What do you mean?"

"Boy…"

It took several seconds for the truth to hit home. "Oh, God, no…"

He stood up and took a step away from me. "Boy…"

"Please!"

I dropped to my knees, covered my face with my hands and cried, but I didn't make a sound.

By the time I looked up, Winston was gone.

So was the Walrus, an hour later, when I'd cried myself out and headed downstairs.

I was sitting in the mausoleum on Thursday morning, staring up at my mom's place on the wall, wiping away tears even before she showed up on the bench next to me.

"My David," she said. "My strong young man."

"Why?"

"David…"

"Don't tell me that I know the answer!"

"But you do," she said.

"I'm going to therapy! Dad and I set it up this morning. I didn't say a word against it."

"Good!"

"Plus, I got Dad to call the Salvation Army," I said. "They're picking up your boxes."

"Good!"

"Plus, we're going to temple on Saturday. We're going to say the *Kaddish* for you."

"David, you know—"

"I know, but we're going to do it anyway. Why can't I keep this one thing? *Please!*"

"That's not how it works," she said.

"But why not? I don't understand."

"You *do* understand, David. You understand in your head but not in your heart. You have to get your head and heart on the same page. Your heart has to understand what your head understands in order to feel better."

"No!"

"Your heart is broken, David. It has to heal."

"No!"

"Here," she said, "take my hand."

"Like at the funeral?" I snapped.

"You were so brave!"

"Dad did it, so I did it. It was his idea."

"But you did it. I was so proud of you."

She put out her hand again, and this time I took it. I held onto her hand, and she led me out of the mausoleum and into the sun. It blinded me at first; that's how bright it was. But then, after a few seconds, my vision came back. I was blinking like crazy, but between blinks, I could see.

"Look at the world, David. That's *your* world."

"All I see is a cemetery," I said.

She let go of my hand and slapped it in a playful way. "Don't be difficult!"

"But that's where we are! That's what I see!"

"That's because you're looking in the wrong direction."

So I looked up. The morning sky was scattered with cotton ball clouds, and the wind was carrying them slowly west to east. Behind them was a blue so deep that I felt like I was swimming in it. But that feeling, that swimming feeling, only lasted for a few seconds. It lasted until I took a breath.

"*That's* your world," she said. "It's lovely and limitless."

"Why can't it be *our* world?"

"It can be our world," she said, "if you make it yours."

"No!"

"*You're* my world, David. You always have been. You always will be."

She pulled me into a hug, and I hugged her back, as hard as I could.

She whispered sweetly, "And you know, we'll always have the Beatles."

We stood in the sun, in the cemetery, and hugged till my arms ached.

About the Author

Mark Goldblatt is the author of the best-selling middle grade novel Twerp and its sequel Finding the Worm, as well as many works of fiction and non-fiction for adults. His writing has appeared in popular and academic journals including the New York Times, Wall Street Journal, New York Post, New York Observer, USA Today, Time, Reason, Commentary, National Review, Quillette, Philosophy Now, and the Sewanee Theological Review. He teaches developmental English and religious history at Fashion Institute of Technology of the State University of New York.

Might as Well be Dead

Lightning Source UK Ltd.
Milton Keynes UK
UKHW021554030323
417988UK00009B/163